T0208526

CINEMATIC IMMUNITY

CINEMATIC IMMUNITY

MATTHEW ROWLAND

CINEMATIC IMMUNITY

iUniverse books may be ordered through booksellers or by contacting:

iUniverse
1663 Liberty Drive
Bloomington, IN 47403
www.iuniverse.com
1-800-Authors (1-800-288-4677)

ISBN: 978-1-5320-9081-3 (sc)
ISBN: 978-1-5320-9082-0 (e)

Library of Congress Control Number: 2019920629

Print information available on the last page.

iUniverse rev. date: 02/11/2020

For Jim —

"a nine to five man who has seen poetry"

Seamus Heaney
The Journey Back

Monday, High Noon

He. Fiftyish, white, male, native Angeleno. Half awake. Out of it. Mostly.

Finds at his door, on the front porch of his house, a young, very attractive black woman.

Him: Confused.
Her: Smiling.

Smiling? Does he know her?

He knows he would like to know her.

Left. Right. Her. Him. Them.
Dry, dusty, deserted neighborhood.
Picture tumbleweeds.
Okay, not tumbleweeds exactly. We aren't talking boonies.
But a red flag warning. 'Course there's always a red flag warning.
It's fuckin' LA.

High noon.
White man, black woman.
A Mexican standoff?

Why is there a bike on his porch?
Something about that. He quakes.

Slightly.

He's scared.

Slightly.

Of what?

A bike?

She reaches out and presses the palm of her hand to his chest. He looks down at her hand.

He thinks.

Anything could happen.

That's the setup.

Early Me to Monday Me

Let me give you a little backstory before we cut to the chase.

First thing is obvious: him is me. Second thing, not so obvious: I do my own stunts.

That might seem strange coming from a man on the wrong side of fifty who's never made it his life's ambition to turn into some mayfly of physical perfection, all six-packs and massive guns and quarter-off-my-ass gluts, but it isn't strange in the mind-set of this Me, your average, F-150, red-blooded American male, strong as he ever was,

Correction,

as he needs to be to get the job done, any job, anytime—still holding steady at his high school middle linebacker primo self, thirty-plus years on from the state finals. Rock-solid at six one and a solid two hundred pounds—if you don't count the dunlap. Plenty enough gas in the tank to do my own stunts. Metaphorically speaking.

How's that exactly?

Well, like most "Me's" I know, when I say stunts, I don't mean *stunt* stunts. I don't mean the professional stuff like jumping off a dam in *The Fugitive* or strapping myself to the outside of a plane like *Mission Impossible* or even selfish amateur gags that those lost man-boys do to get their rocks off on YouTube. No, I don't do any of that. I'm not dumb enough to put my life on the line to pay the bills or jump off a roof to get a laugh.

I am—was—a grip, a key grip. Grips, for those of you who don't know, are just your regular-working everyman, your below-the-line crew stiff at the beating heart of every movie. We're the movers and the builders, not the show-offs flexing their muscles in front of the camera. Those are the stunt guys. Stunt guys flex. I help. 'Course, nowadays, I am flexing a different muscle, the creative one. You see, I've turned screenwriter, which is above-the-line, not below-the-line-working stiff—no more everyman. So, when I say stunts, I mean what the typical status quo–loving, white, middle-aged American male has always done his whole manly life: slide down the knife's edge between stupid and dangerous.

And, no, I'm not talking about eating peanut butter off a spoon straight out of the jar, although I do that too. My stunts are stuff that has to be done for the good of my family, my community—fuck—for the good of us all, just maybe not the way I do it.

Like the time I got up on an overfilled recycling bin to stomp down the cardboard boxes and ended up flat on my back in the driveway. Coulda cracked my head open and bled out on the asphalt. Or the time I decided the best way to get rid of the Christmas tree was to shove it in the fireplace and put a match to it. The chimney practically exploded. Coulda burned the house down and killed the entire family. Or the time … well, you get the idea, just your everyday, life-threatening male stupidity that manly men can't seem to find the horse sense to avoid. Not the need—the needs have to be met. No one's questioning that. Just the how.

Let me say in my own defense that it's not like I'm incapable of thinking through the likely consequences of me just doing me, but sometimes, life doesn't give you any choice. I mean you gotta do what you gotta do, and it's not like there are a whole bunch of stunt guys or riggers hanging around waiting for a chance to double you or clip on a safety line. And, no, I haven't forgotten my age or how my joints ache in the morning. Metaphorically, I'm a minimum-wage bellhop carrying a lifetime's worth of baggage. I know that, and some days, I know it more than others.

But, hey, I'm not the only one who hates getting old. Or the only one who hates to admit what we all know is fact: that sooner or later, it'll be someone else's turn in the sun. Someone younger, stronger, more tech savvy, maybe even smarter. Doing all the stunts, on set and off. Most days, working stiffs like me hope it will be our son slapping our rump and putting us out to pasture, but then, some nights, we wake up knowing it will be a stranger's punk kid who's not filling them even but throwing our shoes in the garbage like they're worthless, like we're garbage too.

Which is actually the trouble. How'd you like being landfilled under that kind of judgment?

I mean, just because I fight being an old shoe, that doesn't mean I'm a bad guy. Just because I look and act like a dinosaur, doesn't mean I can't evolve. Embrace a better me even. Sure, there are guys out there who can't, but they ain't me. Like I tell my kids, if you give me half a chance, if you don't make me a prisoner of my ways, I can get there. Like Jesus said—accept the things you cannot change, have the courage to change some things, blah, blah, blah. You know, camel through the eye of a needle, gospel. And I'm up for it, long as my changing gets me somewhere, long as it doesn't bring my entire life crashing down around my ears.

'Course there's more to me than stunts. Although what comes next might be considered by some as just a stunt. And not in a nice way.

You'll recall I mentioned that after twenty-plus years gripping and getting to the top of that game, I'm taking a crack at screenwriting. How's that? How does a guy who couldn't see the point of high school, let alone college, who always chose working with his hands over reading and writing, think he's got what it takes to make something out of words?

Well, okay, I'd be the first to admit that this is a re-skill, but even that's a bit of a stretch. But that's what makes this country great, right? Opportunity knocks, you grab its ass. That's all I'm doing. What everyone does. Walk through whatever door opens. My open door's name happens to be Shemahn.

That's right, the celebrity Shemahn. She saw something she liked in me one cold, dark night. So now I'm doing my best to bring something, anything into the light.

'Course all the writer's workshops in the world can't make up for what don't come natural. In my own defense, I'll say I've always lived and breathed movies, always loved sitting in the dark watching 'em; love a movie once, love it over and over's my motto. Plus, I also get a kick hearing what the stars are up to. Not in a *People* or *National Enquirer* kind of way. I don't want to know about how some actor's love child is an alien. No, what I like is when actors talk the business, the making ofs. I got a natural curiosity for all things cinematic. Started when I was a kid, and I never grew out of it. What doesn't come natural to me is all the nitty-gritty writer stuff: realistic characters, masterful dialogue, gripping action, happy endings, the made-up, imaginary crap. I'm not talking quips and wisecracks. That I can handle. But trust me, a pile of wisecracks doesn't make a movie. You might not know it, but sitting in a dark movie theater isn't the same as dreaming up tentpoles or franchises or miniseries, but what the heck, right? There's the open door. And even if I don't have what it takes, I'm gonna give it my best shot. Even if jumping into screenwriting's kind of like how I jumped up on that garbage can.

If you're imagining me bleeding out on an empty page, don't hold your breath. I'm not there yet. Sure, I'll admit I'm having trouble keeping my balance. Maybe I'll choke on the next spoonful of peanut butter. Maybe, maybe not, but no matter what, I'm not giving up. I know I'll find what I'm looking for somehow, somewhere. I can't let myself get discouraged.

That's why I started working out of the house. I couldn't take the office. And not because of distractions: commotions, phones ringing, assistants, comings and goings. 'Cause I don't have those. Commotions, assistants, comings and goings, the like. And, yes, I do have internet. And Wi-Fi. So, it's not that. It's the opposite.

At my office, the phone never rings unless it's my Ex. The door never opens if it ain't me coming back from the bathroom. When I'm there, I'm alone with the *tick tick tick*, staring at the computer screen or out the window, telling myself I'm developing character arcs and devising third acts when really all I'm thinking about is why the phone never rings and the door never opens. No one can work like that. Waiting sucks all the creative juices out of a guy, but I'm not worried. I know I'll get back to the office eventually. That's a promise I'm making to myself.

Why have an office if you're not going to use it? Why waste the money? Simple. It's not a waste. And not just because it's my beacon of light in the darkness but because if there's one true thing in Hollywood, you gotta look like success to have a shot at it. It's the same way you have to pretend to believe your own hype. Got to have a name on a door somewhere, some way to say to the wide world, "I'm in the game!" One of these days, there will be someone knocking on the door, and you'll be there to show them the screenplay waiting on your desk.

You'd think things would be different. That instead of grinding on the why nots, instead of avoiding my office, I'd have my feet up on the desk, wheeling and dealing. After all, I've got Shemahn, the attachment that can finance any picture. But I can't wheel or deal without a concept or an inkling of one. What I wouldn't give for a pitch I could just fill in the blanks on: *Top Gun* meets *Old Yeller*. *Gone with the Wind* meets *War of the Worlds*. A pitch of blatant genius could definitely unblock me. Most writers in town are hunting for a star for their project. Me, I'm hunting a sure thing for my star.

'Course, as it turns out, I had it backward. The sure thing was actually hunting me. Remember the setup: him, her,

her hand on his chest. Him is me. She, the sure thing, had tracked me down to my two-bedroom bungalow in Mar Vista.

The bungalow has history too—family history. That's part of this. Hearth and home. The back-backstory. Family. The nuclear one. And I mean that in both senses of the word: the together and the blown-up version of the wife and two kids. Yes, mine is currently postapocalyptic: the Ex is better off happily single, and neither of my kids is talking to me— but not for the same reason. Get a load of this. My daughter thinks of me as a sadly naive Sanjuro from *Yojimbo*. My son thinks the opposite: I'm a wannabe Bryan Mills from *Taken*. Past my sell-by date for her and entirely lacking in those "certain skills" for him. Kinda rock and a hard place, right? 'Course if you ask me, I way prefer Toshiro Mifune's version of *Cinema Man* to Liam Neeson's.

Now you're probably wondering how what my kids think of me now could have nuked my marriage ten years ago. Short answer is not at all. Long answer is it's complicated.

The Ex and I married young, early twenties, basically kids, both starting out in our movie careers. Although, in my Ex's case, starting out looked a whole lot like having it made. Nothing against her and her hairdressing talent, but it didn't hurt coming from Hollywood makeup royalty. Debbie Fisher practically potty-trained my daughter;

Gregory Peck was an honorary godfather to our son. For Christ's sake, we had celebrities coming out our ears. You get the picture. Sure, my Ex's father wasn't a Westmore—and her mother wasn't a Salad Sister—but she had a hairstyling pedigree that predated Technicolor. 'Course she also had her personal infectious can-do. That was how and why I fell in love with her, I guess, watching her bustling around to keep the talent happy. Rain or shine, she never stopped smiling—or flirting. Settling in on an apple box to watch her do final touches was the highlight of my day. And even though I was a third grip making half her hourly, she didn't say no when I asked her out. Maybe like Shemahn she saw something in me. Or maybe no just wasn't in her vocabulary. Till I asked the wrong question that is. I'll get to that.

We bought the Mar Vista place when we were pregnant with our daughter, Hildy. Yup, straight out of *His Girl Friday*. Rosalind Russell was a friend of the family. Maybe we should have waited to start the family till after we'd been married a while, but waiting never occurred to us. We were both working steady; I'd bested a couple of gigs, so I had a career. She was in the contracts of some A-list actors: the kinds of stars who let her pick and choose her gigs, stars who loved that she brought her kid to work.

Between us, we had the dough for a nanny, but the Ex liked having Hildy around, which meant taking her to work most days, which also meant we saw a lot of each other. But then those salad days ended when it was time to have another one and the Ex decided she'd rather stay home and raise the kids. Problem was the Mar Vista place was too small without adding a room. It would have been nice to stay on the Westside, close to the beach, but we couldn't afford it and didn't want to wait on a remodel. So we took out a jumbo mortgage, found ourselves a four-bedroom place with a pool in Simi, and held onto the bungalow for the rental income. We could get by as long as I worked steady, which I did. Started keying, got bigger and bigger shows. Piling up the swag. The American dream, right? But only if that dream is to turn into a workaholic husband, absentee father, to suck at counseling and end up divorced. Not my dream.

Anyhow, after a few years of us headed in different directions, we split. The Ex kept the big house in Simi, and I moved back to Mar Vista. That was good for both of us: it wasn't me getting the short end of the stick. We didn't have one of those ugly divorces. I accepted my fate.

And I didn't hold it against her that when I wanted to add another bedroom so that both kids could stay over, things went sideways. I found out after I'd started the remodel that the house had a crappy foundation, which made it pretty much a teardown. I should have stopped, bulldozed, and rebuilt it right, but I didn't have the cash. Instead, I just kept going, which was dumb, but I didn't know the cheapo contractor I'd hired had screwed me by using crappy Chinese drywall that made everyone sick, including my son, Atticus—yup, I know, it's a helluva name to saddle a kid with, but my Ex was convinced he couldn't go wrong with it, what with the man himself as honorary godfather. Of course, Atticus hasn't exactly lived up to his name, but I guess that's not really the name's fault.

Anyway, like I was saying, the drywall gave my son such bad headaches and nausea when he slept over that he'd spend the whole night throwing up. I figured out what it was and went after the contractor to fix it, but of course, he'd skipped town. Then the contractor's insurance wanted medical proof that my son didn't have a preexisting condition. I didn't have time for that shit. My family was falling apart. One weekend, I ripped out all of the remodel myself, taking every room I'd updated back to the studs to get the house livable again. It was for me and Hildy—but still not for Atticus. 'Cause whatever poison had been in the new drywall had infected the old part of the house; floors, ceilings, water, air. The whole place smelled like sulfur. You didn't need medical proof for that stink. Still, the insurance company wouldn't pay. So, I sued them for the cost of totaling the house. And they fought it, first bullshitting that I had known the drywall I was getting was crap since the price was in the contractor's bid, then claiming that as I had already removed it, my house had been returned to me in better shape than before since I now had the framing for another room. Christ! The bullshit was endless. Meanwhile, my son refused to come near the place—or me. He told my Ex we both made him sick.

Post-family apocalypse is living by yourself in a construction site. It's not as bad as it sounds. And it's not as stinky either. You can hardly smell the sulfur anymore. 'Course now that I've shifted over to writing and I spend a lot more time here, staring at bare studs and exposed conduits, it's almost as bad as going to my office and waiting for the phone to ring. I've been known to waste a whole day imagining what would happen if I just demoed the goddamn place myself, carrying the studs and beams and joists out the front door and dumping them in the middle of my street until the pile got so big it stopped traffic. I'd be in the news for sure.

Insurance crazed homeowner tears down his own home, realizes American nightmare.

Get one of those consumer advocate reporters to take my case.

Grab my fifteen minutes when I can, right?

That was a pretty depressing thought for someone with opportunity about to knock. Which gets me back to Monday, 10 a.m.

I'm home, on a workday, because I'm always home, just like I'm always suffering from my nonwriter's version of writer's block. Page 1 of my practically greenlit, 100-percent-financeable screenplay is blank.

None down, 120 to go.

I'm in Hildy's room. My laptop is open on her desk, screensaver rolling through my kids' pictures. I'm stretched out on her bed in a heat coma, drifting in and out of consciousness, contemplating her left-behind high school decorations and turning drowsy philosopher over why I still think of it as Hildy's room, her desk, and her bed. Because even though her shit is everywhere, it's shit she'll have to talk to me to reclaim. I mean, how, if it isn't her shit anymore, is it still her room? And whose shit is it then if it isn't hers? I'm going full egghead as I'm dragged completely under. Which is where I stay, in my swag T-shirt from *Manifest Destiny II*, knee-length Oakland Raiders board shorts, in my stocking feet, no underwear, table fan propped up on the footboard blowing right up my crotch, completely unconscious, until a scrabbling noise outside, on the other side of the wall from my head, by the side gate that leads to my backyard, jolts me out of my stupor.

Fuck, I think immediately, there's that fuckin' raccoon again.

Oh, one thing I forgot to mention is that I'm at war with an evil raccoon. At least I think it's a raccoon. I haven't ever managed to see it. Neither have any of the exterminators I've hired, but those guys are fuckin' hopeless. They won't crawl under the house; they won't climb up on the roof. Like setting a Havahart is all it takes to catch an animal as smart as a fuckin' raccoon.

Christ, Havahart's a toy to this motherfucker.

Sorry. I don't mean to curse so much, but this is a sensitive subject for me. I got a scary fuckin' animal rabidding its way toward me, chewing through wires, ripping off siding, destroying what's left of my teardown—and I can't do a fuckin' goddamned thing about it.

Sorry! Sorry!

I drum the wall with my open palms to scare it away, accidentally ripping down Hildy's poster of Britney Spears's "Oops! ... I Did It Again" in my clumsy freak-out. The poster was probably a collector's item, but I can't help it. I need to make a lot of noise. I prefer scaring the raccoon away to going mano a mano with a gigantic, vicious, rabid wild animal with fangs and razor sharp claws. I may do my own stunts, but I don't work with animals, particularly wild ones. And the drumming did silence it. Of course, silence on the other side of the wall isn't always a good thing. It means I have to go out and check the damage.

I stagger out of the Hildy's room toward the back door, arming myself with my putter on the way, but before I make it to the kitchen, the doorbell dongs. From where I stand, I see a shadow of a head in the frosted glass of the window light. It's not a UPS ring-and-run; there's someone there. I have to choose, and naturally, given that like most Americans I'm scared to death of the known unknown, I choose the less frightening option and answer the door.

High Noon, 10:02 a.m.

Him a.k.a. me: white man, heat stunned. Out of it.

Her: black woman, young—younger than me anyway—and like I said, very attractive.

She had her back to me, looking out at the street, running her fingers up and down her neck like a pianist practicing her scales. It felt like I was the one who rang her doorbell, who'd dragged her out of her coma, like she would open the door for me when she was good and ready. I'd been around enough women in my life to know their tricks for getting your attention. Making a man wait for you to notice him was one of the best.

Then she turned around, ducked her head, pretending to be embarrassed to find me watching her—another good trick for raising a man's temperature—and kept her eyes down as she struggled to undo the clasp on her helmet.

This damn thing is so tight

She said

Sorry, it's brand-new.

Take your time, I thought.

She wasn't beautiful in a cliché way—nothing as ordinary or fleeting as that. Nothing so common as burning hot and flaming out. Because she wasn't a kid; she was a grown woman. How grown, I couldn't tell you, but make no mistake, she was something—something I couldn't quite get a handle on. Maybe it was the way she let me catch glimpses of her crooked little smile, flashed me glints from her big brown eyes, or that she made a deal of not talking to me with her bike helmet on. A real-life cross between Foxy Brown and Lara Croft: fit, smart, earnest but very sexy and with secrets and loyalties all her own. She's just using her natural talents to get my attention, I thought, and then I got excited to find out why.

When she finally did unsnap the clasp and look up, her smile flatlined: all suggestion, all happy opportunity instantly vanished. She went blank, like she'd only just figured out that I wasn't worth anything, let alone her something. I was about as embarrassed for myself as I'd ever been in my life, wishing I'd chosen door number one: monster raccoon.

But, then, even after that, she wasn't done with me. Her lips pursed; she looked like a cat trying to hide a bird in its mouth.

Yes?

I snapped.

She stared and dug her top teeth deep into her lip. Like she was remembering and enjoying some private joke.

Shame shot from my belly to my eyeballs. My vision fogged. I tried to focus. She seemed familiar. Had we worked together? Was she an actor? Stuntperson? Was she part of Shemahn's entourage? The answer didn't come to me. I bought a little time by throwing a WTF gesture at her bike, but when I raised my eyebrows to demand an explanation, she raised her eyebrows back at me.

I let my chest swell and hiked up my dunlap.

Can I help you?

I'm sorry

She choked on a laugh

I'm sorry … it's just that …

She was smiling her crooked, sheepish smile and pointing at my head.

Right then, I felt the pinch of what was so funny. I had come to the door with my laser hair-restorer helmet on my head. I'd been wearing it when I fell asleep.

No offense … I didn't mean …

She seemed apologetic, but it didn't matter.

On any other day, with any other person, I would have laughed at the situation, because I mean, fuck, it's not like I don't know I've lost my hair, but she had definitely taken all the piss out of me. I pretended I didn't know what she was talking about as I stood, a Colossus astride my threshold.

Even if it was self-inflicted, I didn't like being humiliated in front of a beautiful woman, even one who barely had any hair herself, since her own copper brown curls were shorn close to her scalp.

I'm on a deadline. Maybe you could call my office and speak to my assistant.

Without any warning, she reached out and put the palm of her hand in the middle of my chest, fingers spread over the "Manifest" in *Manifest Destiny*.

Samson Agonistes

She said.

Samson's not my given name but I didn't correct her. I looked down at her hand, felt her skin through my T-shirt.

We need to talk.

As if on cue, two car doors slammed—

Bam!

Bam!

She looked up and down my street and then over her shoulder at the houses behind us. Her hand did not move. She leaned into me.

Could we go inside?

All her Lara Croft confidence and Foxy Brown wiles were calling forth panic and fear in me.

I have no idea who you are

I said

or why you're touching me.

She snatched her hand back like she'd been burned.

Of course. Of course. Please let's start over. My name is Petunia Biggars, and I would like to apologize ... about you know ... the hair-restorer thing ...

What was I missing? Were we back to her wanting something from me that I would be excited by? No. No way. Why would a beautiful African American woman want to have anything to do with me? It couldn't be that. Something wasn't right. She looked up and down the street again. She seemed scared.

I followed her look, feeling the grab of the hair helmet's edge on the short hairs of my neck. Tears stung my eyes. I blinked away the weakness. The street was empty and quiet. We could have been the last two humans on earth, but I had no intention of being rolled. Total stranger pushing herself into my house? No way. I put my hand on the doorjamb. It wasn't hard to convince myself the whole thing was a setup, that Petunia Biggars—or whatever her real name was—was just the bait for the honey trap, that there was a gang loose in my neighborhood looking for suckers who'd fall face-first into her sticky sweetness while they were being stung in the ass.

I'm sorry. I'd really like to help, but ...

She gripped her helmet in front of her chest like a shield

You would feel differently if you knew what was really going on. Of the evil forces at work.

I would, I thought. Everybody would. That was exactly the problem with this situation: I still didn't know what was really going on with her. Maybe what she was really scared of was getting the crap beaten out of her for not conning her way inside my house.

Look, I don't know how you know me, or if I know you, but if you're really in danger, you'd be better off going to the police.

Not just me—you're up to your neck in this too.

Really? I scanned the street and still did not seeing anything scary.

Look, I appreciate you warning me, if that's why you're here, but if you don't mind, I'm really busy. But I would tell you that

For some reason, even though I'd just told her how busy I was, I started blathering on like a complete jackass

I've found in life, and I recommend, by example, since we're kind of exchanging boons, kindness of strangers et al., you warning me, me giving my honest reaction to you, that it works better for most people, including yours truly, when I'm allowed to decide for myself what I'm up to my neck in and whether I want to put the aforementioned neck on the line to save the neck of someone I've never met before.

Maybe it was the nonsense, maybe it was the hair helmet, but she really let me have it. All the smiles were gone. She turned on a dime from frightened to fucking mad.

What? You out of the white savior business now that you've lost your hair? Shame. Too bad there's no miracle treatment that can restore a man's basic humanity. Or are you just too fragile to give what's really needed instead of what you imagined? Either way seems the world's out one savior. All that's left is an old bald man can't be bothered to save a poor little black girl who's actually trying to save him.

She cut me deep, hari-karied me from my manhood to my gut. Not that I could process whether she was right about me. She took a breath. Looked at me harder than I've been looked at in a long time. Me being me, I start talking before my mind catches up with my mouth.

Like *Heat of the Night* or *To Sir, with Love*, Poitier is classic fish out of water, but he still changes all those racist minds.

Do I look like a fish out of water to you?

She asked.

No, I thought. I didn't have any words other than that, but I did have action. I swung my putter out in front of me like Excalibur. Like that would mean she couldn't deny who I was: Samson. I was still Samson. Like whoever was out there threatening us would see that they would have their hands full, but even I could imagine how lame I looked in my movie swag and hair helmet, more cosplay than superhero.

You're welcome to sit out here.

I swung my putter toward the swing the Ex and I had put on the east end of the porch for our prechild utopian cocktails.

While you wait for the cops.

I tried to keep things light.

Be careful though. My daughter insists it's not safe … some kind of jinx—

Fuck you and your kindness-of-strangers-white-fragility-Blanche-Dubois bullshit!

She crammed the helmet back on her head and then bolted, sprinting flat out across my yard, hurdling my neighbor's fence, turning hard right down their driveway, and vanishing. I stood there for a while, almost expecting her to appear again on the other side of their house—heading in the opposite direction, perhaps with someone chasing her. I told myself I would help if someone was on her tail. Samson would putt them to smithereens.

She did not reappear. I unflexed.

Then, without my being aware of it, my neighborhood returned to its normal red flag calm, almost like there had never been a Mexican standoff.

A moment later, I heard the sound of another car door slamming. My head jerked reflexively as if someone had bounced a basketball off it, and I felt the pinch of my balding reality on my neck. I ripped the helmet off, slunk back inside, quietly closed the door, and then, even more quietly, locked all the locks.

So, you're thinking, back to the setup:

White man, black woman, all alone in the middle of a stifling, red flag heat wave.

So how did anything happen the way it did or end the way it did, me being able to help her, almost helping her, then not?

Was she right? Was I the problem? Was it really my white savior's way or the highway when you knocked on my door?

I didn't want to believe that's what it was.

I mean, how could it be that the stranger asking for help was more in the right than the person who didn't have a clue what was going on? She wasn't bleeding. She wasn't lying unconscious by the side of the road. She had a top-of-the-line bike. Why should I be so trusting? We didn't live in a Saturday morning cartoon. We lived in a world where bad people, some of whom are beautiful women, tried to sucker others into trusting them. I remembered how not so long ago criminals used to get gullible old people tied up in a long conversation at the front door while they sent their accomplices 'round the back. Had they targeted me because they thought I was old? I *had* been getting mailers from the AARP.

Just like that, I convinced myself I had dodged a bullet. She'd been playing on my liberal guilt, but I'd kept my head. I wasn't fooled by my attraction to her either. I went around the house, locked the doors and windows, closed all the blinds, and set my burglar alarm. Even in an unbearable red flag heat, even in a teardown, I'd rather not make myself a sitting duck. Clearly, someone had wanted something from me. I doubted it was to sell me a Bible.

Looking back on things, hindsight and all, of course it was a mistake not to have helped Petunia. Because in hindsight she wasn't lying about the danger to all of us. So, it disappoints me that I let my bruised manhood keep me from trusting that. And when I said before that anything could happen, I meant that almost rhetorically, if you know what I mean, like a rhetorical question. I mean, considering who I am, could anything really have happened, all in all things considered?

Not that I had time for that debate. I went back to Hildy's room. Hunkered down in my own sweat, I tapped the space bar on my laptop with a dripping finger as I sat down in her desk chair and put my socked feet up on her bed. As I waited for the computer to wake up, I remembered that I hadn't done anything about the raccoon. I grabbed the putter and ripped open the back door, forgetting that I had just set the alarm, which meant a mad scramble through the house, slipping and sliding on the wood floors, punching my code into the keypad seconds before the alarm went off. On my way, I'd put my left foot through a cabinet door in the dining room and caught the big toe of my right foot on the heating grate. So, there were consequences. I didn't think my toe was broken, but it was throbbing as I limped out the back door in my socks, swinging my putter and preparing myself for a fight to the death.

Fight with my imagination was more like it. There was no raccoon and no sign of one, not even in the bushes near my daughter's window. I circled the house, on the lookout for damage and danger, and banged on the siding with one hand while wielding the putter in the other as I advanced against the known unknown. It wasn't until I got around to my front yard that I saw anything out of the ordinary. Even then, it wasn't so much a surprise as a revelation: Petunia Biggars's bicycle was still sitting on my porch. She'd run off without it.

And that was how I knew I'd fucked up. You see, that bike was the sign I had not seen before.

How could a bike convince me of something that a scared young woman could not? How could a bike bring me to my senses?

This is how: by being the one thing in this entire anything-could-happen moment that didn't make sense. A honey trap wouldn't ride a bike to the crime scene, would she? Wouldn't bring it up on my porch as if it could not be out of her sight? A honey trap wouldn't then run off and leave her bike behind, would she?

No. It was clear. This bike mattered. It would have to be saved.

It was a real beauty in any case, one of those electric ones that you see whizzing all over the bike path in Santa Monica, one that makes you jealous of the young tech hotshots and their fantastic girlfriends, brand-new without much wear on the tires or any nicks in the frame. It smelled like it had just come off the floor. Almost like the first time Petunia had ridden it was over to my house. That's the reason she was so protective, you're thinking, but you'd be wrong. There was one more thing: the basket on the front of it, ordinary, appropriate to the bike in every way save one. It was wrapped around and around and around in a heavy, rubber-coated black chain and fastened with a ridiculously huge padlock. It looked like one of those fantasy treasure chests buried under an X marks the spot.

The bike said it all: Petunia had been and was in real danger. And so was I, but I was too busy stepping on my own dick to hear the warning. I'd as good as shot the messenger. What happened to all my openness to change? I hated the idea that she might have been right about me being the problem more than I hated not living up to my nickname, but then I thought, it might be too late to save us both. Maybe saving her bike and whatever was in the basket from the evil forces would be enough. Till she came back. Because I had to believe she would be back.

I wheeled her bike around the house and up the kitchen steps, through the patio doors, and into the dining room. I put it on the side of the table next to the window where it would be out of the way but safe. It would be waiting for her when she found her way back to my door. I had faith. I had to. I couldn't contemplate any other alternative. Foxy meets Lara—Petunia Biggars was formidable. She was something. Much more something than a balding Samson that's for sure.

And until she came back for her treasure, I would hope for the best and try not to dwell on the mistake I had made. I checked all the locks, set the alarm again, and went back to what I'd been doing before the doorbell rang: lying on my daughter's bed, not writing my screenplay. You might think that was morally the wrong thing to do. That I should have been calling the cops or driving around looking for her, but life doesn't work like that. You can't always fix your mistakes by pretending to do something useful. People who show up at your door aren't like lost dogs running around in circles at your feet.

With people, you have to wait for them to find their way back to you.

Monday, 3:00 p.m.

Come back, Petunia! Come back!

I was calling out in my sleep.

Petunia?

A woman responded.

Halfway awake, I burped up my last meal: BBQ chips and grocery store egg salad. I felt hot and clammy. Both sick and not sick.

That sounds like one weird-ass dream, Sam. I never had you figured for a Shirley Booth wannabe. Or maybe it's a little dog you're missing. Are you lonely? Do you need a friend?

My Ex was staring at me from the end of the bed. Fuck, I thought. What's she doing here?

You're thinking that most people would have had the locks and alarm changed to prevent such surprises, but like I said, it wasn't that kind of divorce. I put my forearm over my eyes.

Dog or no dog. It's three in the afternoon. Get up.

I did not budge. It was not because I doubted her temporal awareness but because I didn't have anything to get up for. I hadn't come unblocked, and Petunia hadn't come back for her bike.

I'm sure you appreciate the irony of this

She said.

I could feel the breeze made by her arm waving, but I didn't open my eyes to see what the *this* was that she was referring to. All I could think about was how goddamned hot it was and wondering what had happened to my fan.

It's no wonder you can't get anyone to go to bed with you.

This was an insult too far, but I did not give her the satisfaction of acknowledging it.

Look at you, lying in your daughter's tweener bedroom in the middle of the day, completely naked, probably hungover, wearing some knockoff laser hair-restorer helmet. Holy cow, Samson, at your age, you'd think you'd have the decency not to inflict your male vanity on the unsuspecting Philistines.

Go to hell!

I sat up to pull a sheet over my privates before whipping the helmet into the closet. I changed the subject.

You aren't a Philistine. And you're not allowed to call me Samson anymore. No one is.

Except for Petunia Biggars I made a mental note. For now anyway. Even if didn't seem right that someone I'd never met before was calling me by a nickname that had a complicated history. I would have to mention that when she thanked me for saving her bike.

My name is actually Samuel Agonistes. Sam for short. Not Samson. I'm not just being a dick when I ask people to stop calling me that. Samson's the nickname I got playing middle linebacker in high school. Big and strong, remember? And unstoppable. I would bust through blocks and make tackles with guys hanging off of me. Like that *Blindside* guy. Although I was never gonna go pro. Never that good. Just good enough to carry my team to the state championship. 'Course I couldn't win it for 'em, but almost. Game went into the final minutes tied 0–0. Then our QB cracked under the blitz and threw a stupid interception, their DB ran it in, and we lost 6–0. So not a state champ, but still Samson, which I admit I liked more than a little. I mean, who wouldn't want to be the guy who gets called to the rescue, the guy who gets people out of a jam?

'Course, I know it's not as simple as that, that a nickname can cut both ways, can get you in trouble even, in over your head, particularly one with a history like mine. Wine, women, and song—what have you? Not that everyone knows the whole story of the original Samson—I would say mostly they don't—except for the strength part. So when it comes to me, it's pretty clear: either they call you by your nickname because they love you and appreciate your strength or they call you that because they think you're actually weak and are just trying to push your buttons. With family and friends it can be both things at the same time. But with people in the business, particularly above-the-lines, to them Samson's almost always a joke, a relic, a reason to ignore me. Which is why I'm trying to put it behind me.

But don't go thinking you're the only one who got the joke

I said. I was not done with my Ex.

There was another woman who picked up on the helmet irony before you.

Someone you could have been sleeping with if you hadn't been wearing it?

The Ex was not done with me.

Fat chance. She's probably fifteen years younger than me and quite out of my league.

Old men exposing themselves is out of fashion.

I wasn't naked.

Helmets aren't technically clothes.

I'm pretty sure I had on a T-shirt and board shorts and socks.

If it was your normal over-the-hill jock wear, that's worse than a helmet.

She picked up the foot of the bed and slammed it on the floor.

Get up! You're going to miss your call.

Screenwriters don't have a call.

But fathers do. Get up and get dressed!

She grabbed my feet and started pulling.

I held onto the headboard with one hand and the sheet covering my junk with the other.

What the fuck is your problem? I can walk around naked in my own home. The blinds are closed. No one can see me, but even if they could, I'm a writer. Writers are supposed to be eccentric.

You don't get to be eccentric today.

What are you even doing here in the middle of the afternoon? Shouldn't you be busy printing money? Does Elizabeth know you're playing hooky?

Elizabeth was her boss, a whiz kid science geek. They found each other at an Oscar party. My Ex, as it turned out, was an honest-to-goodness smarty-pants. Top of her class non-traditional business undergrad, night school MBA. Now the CFO for the latest Silicon Beach unicorn. Company did Crispy … Crisper something. Everybody said what they were doing was the next big thing in medicine. My Ex ran the business side of the joint; she was also the human touch. Although I wasn't finding her particularly relatable at that moment.

Today, you have to go back to being a grip—until we track down Atticus.

I stopped kicking my feet and opened my eyes.

What happened?

He walked off the set on Friday night. Now he's not answering his phone. Angel called me when he couldn't get you. Tonight, it's all car rigs and exteriors in Long Beach. You have to cover for your son.

What's the call?

Five.

All my rigging gear is rented out. I don't even have a spare set of Allen wrenches.

He just needs '*Samson*'.

She made air quotes, like she could say it because she wasn't the one saying it.

Okay, okay. I'll be in Long Beach in two hours. Have Angel text me the location.

I stood up and pulled the sheet with me as I shuffled toward my bathroom.

And please, for the sake of our happy divorce, cut that Samson crap!

Let me make you a sandwich

She said

I brought groceries.

Put them in the fridge or take them with you. I'll eat off the caterer. Your mothering is done here.

She put her foot on the sheet and snatched it out of my loose grip. I was standing there naked, exposing myself to a mass of one.

Has that laser zapped up what little was left of your grey matter? My work is not done. Yours neither. We have to figure out what's happened to our son. Together. Now we can either talk about this with you holding your closed-for-repairs manhood in your hand or you can get dressed while I fix you something to eat, and then we can sit down at your dining room table and discuss it like the civilized parents we still are. Your choice. Either way, we're talking before you roll out of here.

How delightful!

I said, giving my best buck-naked impression of a civilized man turning the other cheek, ripping off a loud fart and stalking into the bathroom.

Monday Ticking Over to Tuesday, Midnight, First Meal

I'll admit there were moments when I forgot to be unhappy that I was up all night shooting a night exterior, times that I was pumped to be gripping again. It's hard not to like doing something you're good at.

The highlight of it all was shooting the shit with my pal Alexander Nauman, the director of the action unit I was day-playing on. Everyone else was in a hotel ballroom holding area eating "lunch" at midnight. Alex and I weren't hungry enough to make the effort; we were sitting in the dark at camera, swapping war stories and laughing at all the stupid things we'd done over the years.

We went way back, but things being what they were, we hadn't seen each other in a couple of years. Alex was part German and part Mexican, best of both worlds I liked to say, passionately dispassionate, working in Hollywood on one of those genius visas, but basically a real solid guy. He knew what he wanted and knew how to get it. My favorite kind of director.

Alex had heard about what happened with Shemahn, but he wanted the inside story.

Shooting behind the scenes on *The Twilight Zone* is not the same thing as being *on The Twilight Zone*! I can't believe you said that to a director!

Alex couldn't get over that one.

In front of the entire crew?

Fuck no, it was just me and the DP.

Still, I can't believe he didn't fire you on the spot.

Tried. Shemahn threatened to call *Variety* if he did.

Can't blame her. Seems like you were the only one who cared what happened to her.

That's harsh, Alex. We were all doing our best. Even your douchebag first AD. He just didn't see what was coming as clearly as I did.

Alex looked doubtful.

I can't believe that. Even Danny We're-Making-Our-Day-No Matter-What Briscoe?

Sure. Danny just needed a little reminding of his potential, like the Wizard reminded the Scarecrow. I was there handing out safety diplomas for all the—

Right then, the first AD we'd been discussing, Danny Briscoe, parked himself between me and Alex. I hadn't said enough to really incriminate myself but it wouldn't have mattered if I had. Danny was too busy using up all the oxygen in downtown Long Beach to show how important he was to hear anything I said.

Tommy checked all the pouches?

Danny shouted into his walkie-talkie and then stopped yelling to listen.

Okay, well, tell the office that, word for word. Yeah, that's right: word for word. Repeat after me: Tommy checked the pouches on all the director's chairs and the camera truck.

We did all we could do, and we couldn't find his Big Gulp. Next time, he should bring a cup bearer to the set with him.

Danny laughed at his own joke.

Couldn't find what?

Alex wasn't laughing.

Milton's Big Gulp. You know that ginormous silver jug he carries everywhere?

Alex opened his mouth to speak, but Danny raised a hand to stop him. He wasn't done with his conversation on the walkie.

Okay, Molly. Fine. Leave out the cup bearer crack. And sure not word for word. Sure. Say it however you want. We can't find it. End of story. Who gives a fuck?

It's not a Big Gulp, Danny

Alex said

Big Gulps are what *you* drink out of. Milton's cup is engraved with a copy of Rodin's *Gates of Hell*. That's a famous sculpture.

Who the fuck cares what it is? Besides, a man that rich loses something, he sends someone out to buy him another one.

Unique means one of a kind, irreplaceable.

Should be in a museum if it's the fuckin' holy grail of Big Gulps

Danny cracked wise.

Still, you need to find it.

Alex was clear but Danny wasn't listening. He looked at his watch and then keyed his walkie.

So, we're back, people. We're back in!

His yell into his walkie mic broke everyone's eardrums and the comforting dead-of-night peace in the same breath. All around the dark streets, you could hear production assistants echoing him.

We're back in! We're back in!

So, A-Man, same setup: crane on the insert car, free drive low angles?

Alex hated being called A-Man, but all he said was

Yes, Danny. I haven't changed my mind in the past half hour.

Where's Ted, guys? I need him at camera

Danny shouted as he walked off to find the picture car coordinator.

Everybody should be looking for Ted!

Milton, Alex? As in Milton J. Milton?

I was impressed.

Alex smiled.

My wife thinks it might be a deal with the devil, but Milt promises he can get me a feature this year. No more action units.

Fuck. That's great—congratulations!

Hey, Samson?

Danny returned, as full of himself as before, but with a new edge to him. I resisted the temptation to correct him on my name. I guess he figured he could focus on me now that the set was in motion. I was the key grip on his last picture who had embarrassed him by stopping him from killing

Shemahn. Like most firsts, Danny never liked admitting his mistakes—even the ones he hadn't been allowed to make.

I heard you were stalking us, mister.

Danny referred to everyone below him on the food chain as mister.

Day-playing for your son? How's that all-night condor duty suit you?

He enjoyed the image of a former key stuck up in a condor.

No condor duty. Rigs mainly.

You should have seen your baby boy's tantrum the other night. What an asshole!

Yeah? I heard he wasn't acting like himself.

Oh, he was himself all right, a regular piece of work—just like his father. Right, A-Man?

Give it a rest, Danny.

Alex did his best to deflect him, but Danny wasn't done.

With a son like yours, Samson, guess you'll be full-time babysitting. No more celebrity gravy train for you.

If you say so, Danny.

I hauled myself out of the director's chair so that we'd be eye to eye.

A smart key like Angel knows to call me in when there's a blowhard who doesn't know his head from his ass about safety.

Alex blurted out a surprised laugh, which he tried to cover with a cough. He popped up off the peewee dolly and walked off in the direction of base camp.

Catch you later, Alex

I shouted after him.

He had to wave because he was laughing so hard.

Better get to it, eh, Danny? Don't want anyone sayin' I'm a goldbrick.

Fuckin' asshole!

Danny erupted.

Get off my set, you fuckin' has-been! Forget picking up the pieces for your lame-ass son. You won't be able to day-play anywhere in this town when I'm through with you.

I could hear Alex laughing, but none of this was funny to me. I never took pleasure in taking a peg out of a smart-ass AD. Particularly Danny. He wasn't a bad guy, maybe too arrogant. Could be he'd been firsting too long. Maybe he'd let the little power he had go to his head. I wasn't particularly worried that he could keep me from gripping if I wanted to. No first AD could seriously hurt a key with my resume.

Angel agreed with me that it was better that I stay on the forty-footer for the rest of the night. No reason to rub the reality of his limited influence in Danny's face if I didn't have to. Not too hard a gig: cutting speed rail, building rigs, waiting for someone on the radio to call for something off the truck, and then pulling it out onto the tailgate. I was alone with a long six hours ahead of me, but I didn't mind. I had plenty to think about. What? Well, my whole non-nuclear family for starters, but mainly Atticus.

Off the bat, let me say that even though I wanted things for my kids, I never let what I wanted stand in the way of what they wanted. I wasn't a father trying to realize my dreams through his offspring. Mostly, I stayed out of their way and let them be. Tried to want for them what they wanted. Let them have their own ambition. 'Course, that didn't mean I'd let them off the hook if there wasn't any ambition to speak of. I wouldn't let 'em flounder on the dole. I had basic expectations.

Maybe you're thinking it was those expectations that nuked my nuclear family. And you wouldn't be far off if you did. Except that you'd be leaving out the other backfire: the gamble I took with our future. Sometimes referred to by me as the chance of a lifetime.

This guy I knew, another key grip, had this side business renting equipment and trucks to productions. From the outside, it looked like the business made him a ton of dough; how else can you explain him being able to stop gripping altogether, retire, and head down to Mexico to spend the rest of his life sitting on the beach drinking Coronas? It was just my good fortune that since he didn't have kids, retiring for him meant he was looking for someone to buy him out. Someone could've been anyone, but the someone he chose was me.

The Ex and I talked it over. She didn't see it the same way I did. I thought I could build us a real nest egg, create something for our kids. I already had the perfect name: the Samson Family Group. She went over the numbers with a fine-toothed comb and told me best case it was hand-to-mouth.

Maybe it is now

I said

But I'll grow it.

How? What's a key grip who hates math and never went to college know about growing a business?

Trust me

I said

A man like me isn't scared of what he doesn't know.

And that's all she wrote

She smart-assed me.

But all I was thinking was: he's a key, I'm a key. Fuck the math! How hard could it be?

Long story short, even though her answer was no, she let me borrow the money to buy him out.

How hard could it be? Pretty damn hard is what I found out. The Ex was right: I didn't know the first fuckin' thing about running a business let alone growing one. And, of course, there were problems coming down the road that guy I bought it from hadn't pointed out to me—if he'd even seen 'em. Those problems meant I had to keep keying or have hand-to-mouth turn into completely belly-up.

To her credit, even though I'd put our future at risk, the Ex never said I told you so. Never said anything in fact. 'Course she never turned her can-do to my problem either. What was the point? Like she said, all she wrote had been written. No use in both of us bleeding out on the pavement.

Our problem was my problem. Her problem was looking after her own future, which did not mean her going back to hairstyling. What it meant was going back to school and getting busy on her own nest egg. A real one. And a new nest too—one with no room for me.

Big surprise, Samson Family Group didn't help me much with my kids either. I'd renamed the company and put family in the title 'cause that's the way I saw it: as something that would bring us closer. I figured it'd be fun to have the kids work there in the summer and if either one liked it enough and was as good as their mom with business and numbers, they could take it over completely one day; it ain't hard to imagine how a family business could satisfy all our ambitions.

And Hildy and me, we did have fun. For the first couple of years anyway. Things changed some when I had to start gripping more to make ends meet. I wasn't around a lot, and business was slow; there wasn't much to do. She didn't like being stuck in an office so much after that. And she didn't like being her brother's boss. He was always screwing up, sending out the wrong equipment, forgetting orders, and smoking weed on the roof. She hated having to discipline him. She hated pretending that he should be working when there was no work to do. She started grinding on me to let her come on the set and grip with me. Be an intern or my apprentice. That idea took some getting used to; I mean, there weren't a lot of female grips around. And by the time I did get used to it, Hildy had changed her mind. She had found her ambition. She wouldn't be taking over Samson Family Group after all. She was going to go to college to become a veterinarian.

And at the age of twenty-seven, that's what she was: a veterinarian with her own small clinic. Had to take out a hefty loan to do it, but she did. Okay, so, she was pissed at me about not giving her the money, making her borrow it instead from a bank, but try to see it my way before you jump down my throat. Okay, sure, her mom had mostly paid for college and vet school, so it wasn't like I'd been stretched up to that moment, but the truth was I was barely scraping by.

What about a second mortgage?

I'd love to honey, but I can't do anything legal with this house until the insurance pays off. And you know how things are with the business.

She was disgusted.

Dad, it's been seven years since you were fucked on this remodel, and you haven't seen a dime. How long are you going to hold us all hostage to this teardown? And SFG? That's not a business—that's a black hole. Any accountant could tell you that, but you know what I think? I think it's not about you not being able to come up with the cash. I think it's about paying me back for not working with you at Samson, about me kicking your family business pipedream in the balls.

And maybe she was right. Maybe I was mad at her for rejecting the opportunity I could provide, but I didn't stop her, did I?

And as I said, she got her loan—just not from her father— which was probably better for her in the long run, right? Better to learn how to jump through life's hoops sooner rather than later. Because there's no end to the hoops. A Shemahn comes along once in a blue moon, but hoops will always be with us. So, in my mind, staying out of her way worked just fine.

I wish I could say the same for my son. It was a lot more complicated with him. His name was just the tip of the iceberg.

When our first kid turned out to be a girl, my Ex told me her name was gonna be Hildy. I didn't exactly get rolled, but my opinion didn't count. That was more or less okay with me since I liked the name. I considered it kind of a blessing from the stars. My daughter would live up to her celebrity guardian angel and turn out smart and tough and beautiful. Like Rosalind Russell. Like my Ex.

So, when our second kid turned out to be a boy, I had the idea that I'd get more say, that I could put my foot down and get a Sam Junior out of the deal. No way. The Ex didn't mind the Samuel, but Junior was a nonstarter. And remember, she insisted that we get some nod to Greg Peck in there. Greg Peck as Atticus Finch that is. Not as Ahab. Or Mengele. Peck would be the boy's celebrity guardian angel. And my Ex thought Atticus was Greek enough to sound good with Agonistes. So, we named him Samuel Atticus Agonistes. And so there wouldn't be any confusion by him being called Sammy or Sam and having my name and not being junior or the second, she decided we'd call him Atticus.

You may think that sounds a little screwy, but hold on, I'm not finished. The whole thing took a turn for the worse in seventh grade. Atticus had been doing mock trial as his extracurricular, and his team with our boy as the star of the defense had just made it to the city finals. His mom thought this proved her right—the name was paying off, and her son was destined to be some high-powered lawyer—but then right after they won the whole shooting match, without any warning, Atticus dropped both mock trial and his name.

I hate it

He told my Ex

Everybody teases me about growing up to be a do-gooder just like him.

Could do a lot worse, Atticus

She said and tried to give him a congratulatory hug.

He pushed her away.

No, I couldn't. Don't call me that anymore. It's not who I am.

Atticus is the kind of name that'll get you somewhere, that stands out

I said, even though I was secretly happy that maybe I'd be getting my Sam Junior after all.

But my son didn't buy that argument.

Where's Samson gotten you, Dad?

Samson's not my name. It's a nickname.

Well, Atticus isn't mine anymore.

It'll be confusing to have two Sams in the family

The Ex said.

No, it won't since I'm not gonna be Sam either. I'm Peck.

Peck?

I said

What kind of made up name is that?

A real person's kind of made-up name—unlike Atticus.

I can't call you that

The Ex announced

It sounds like a dirty word. Besides, it's not your legal name.

You can call me whatever you want, but I'm only going to answer to Peck.

And so it was. From that day forward, Atticus was Peck. Not to me or the Ex. We either called him "Atticus" or "son" or nothing—and he didn't seem to care.

Pretty much the only one in the family who would call him Peck was Hildy.

People should be called what they want

She said.

I had to admit she had a point. Plus I was hoping that being called what he wanted would fix things for him. It didn't. They got worse.

In high school, he had a bunch of problems, but the biggest one was he was too smart for his own good. He'd coast through his classes, studying just enough to keep his GPA respectable, somehow acing the big tests, and always looking for an angle that meant he didn't have to exert himself. And as long as he didn't have to work too hard to stay out front, he was a happy kid, fun to be around.

Of course, it wasn't all cream cakes and crates of Pepsi as they say. I mean, there were signs we saw and signs we should have seen. Told ourselves not to sweat the small stuff when we probably should've. One thing we should have sweated was his quitting the soccer team his junior year. It wasn't like with mock trial—quitting when he was on top—he quit soccer because he was riding the bench. He'd lost his spot to a Hispanic kid who had moved to LA from Texas.

The coach said that the boy was a citizen—his parents were illegals, but the kid had been born in the United States—but Atticus didn't believe it, particularly after he saw the kid selling oranges on an off-ramp. Atticus complained to the school but got nowhere. He muttered things about wetbacks but mostly told everyone he didn't want to waste his life on sports, that he had more important things to do with his time, but the Ex and I could see how angry he was.

Then when he didn't get into Berkeley, whatever it was in him that had soured about soccer, really soured for good. Or maybe what had always been rancid just burped out in our faces. He refused to even consider going to college.

What's the use?

He said

The same foreigner who took my spot to fill some bullshit quota will just take my job later on anyway.

At that point, he laughed when he said those kind of things—like he only said them to piss us off—but there was real resentment too. Like he wanted to shove in our faces how he was rejecting the spirit of his name.

The Ex and I were pulling our hair out, trying to figure out what had happened, how such a normal kid had turned out so sour. Because he had been just a regular kid to us. Until he became Peck, and then he wasn't. Like he'd lost his guardian celebrity. Sure, he was always on the lookout for the shortcut to easy street, but that isn't in and of itself too big a problem in life as long as you don't lose your shit when things aren't easy 'cause it turns out there is no shortcut. But Atticus *did* mind. Really minded. It made him seriously angry that *true* Americans were being left behind. For the past couple years, he'd been going through life pretty pissed off, believing other people were getting what they didn't deserve while all his shortcuts led to deadends. And he was too angry to talk to about it. To reason with. Meanwhile, all the Ex and I could do was hope he'd grow out of it.

One day, he came and asked me to help him get into gripping. Truth is I was surprised. Not that I didn't want him working with me. Remember SFG? I had him working there in the summers even after Hildy quit, but then he fucked up so many times, I had to fire him. I suppose I should have known gripping was another case of him taking a shortcut, but it didn't appear that way at first.

The Ex and I were happy. Our boy was finally getting his head on straight. He had a new girlfriend—a nice Asian girl, a dental hygienist he'd met online, so maybe he was over the foreigner thing—and he wanted to move out of his mother's house, which meant he needed a job. Gripping was good money. Why not use his connections like everyone else did? I was happy to help. Atticus seemed grateful. My former best boy-turned-key grip, Angel, did me a solid. My boy had been on his crew for more than a year, and things were mostly good. Sure, I heard that he had some attitude and that people were only putting up with his shit because of me. I had to intervene a couple of times and set the kid straight, but I hadn't heard any complaints in a while. I thought things were settling down. Driving to Long Beach in bumper-to-bumper traffic, I figured all I had to do was soothe Angel's ruffled feathers and set my boy back on the straight and narrow.

Unfortunately, that was just the half of it.

Angel waited till after wrap, till the forty-footer was buttoned up and his guys were walking away; he tossed me an egg sandwich and sat down on the curb. I knew from the slump in his shoulders that he couldn't quite figure out how to say what he had to say. I watched the craft service guys sweeping the street in front of us as I bit into my sandwich. If there was one thing I missed about night exteriors, it was a hot bacon and egg sandwich at wrap.

How many days you got left on this?

I said, through a mouth full of bread and fried egg.

Two. We're off tomorrow and Wednesday, turning around for a day call for some first-unit pickups with Jesse. Bunch of tight shots and new driving scene with some wannabe actress.

Got anything coming up?

Start prep week Monday on *MD7: Shit Hits Fan*.

I laughed.

Can't believe that *Manifest Destiny* franchise is still on its feet.

Me either. Remember, on the first one, the two of us wondering who would actually pay to see this crap?

We shook our heads at Hollywood craziness. I finished my sandwich and balled up the wrapper. I could feel Angel getting up the courage.

I'm not going to be able to take Peck with me on *MD7*.

Because of the other night? I get it. Seems fair.

I accepted that there had to be some consequences for his fuckup.

Well, yes ... partly ... but it's not just *MD7*.

Angel leaned away from me like we were both the negative poles of a magnet.

Spit it out, Angel.

I don't want you to take it wrong. You're too good a friend …

Yes, I am a good friend, and, yes, you may say something to piss me off, but if you don't say whatever you brought me down to Long Beach to say, it's definitely going to push me over the edge.

The guys and I can't work with your kid anymore—and I can't dump him on other union keys either.

I thought for a moment about my son washing out as a grip and wondered if it was a sign of his washing out in general.

Is he just no good? Not strong enough?

Oh, no. It's not that. He's good enough, strong enough. I could see him going nonunion and picking up extra man-days here and there.

What is it then?

It's more of a people thing.

Okay?

It was clear I didn't know what a people thing was.

Stuff he says, how he reacts to situations, how me makes people—actors—uncomfortable …

What do you mean exactly? You can't really take away someone's livelihood for making people uncomfortable.

Samson, 1 know it's gotta be tough to hear this from anyone—and maybe it's worse coming from a friend. I thought I owed you the truth, but if you'd rather not, we can—

Okay, you're right. I'll shut up.

Angel took a deep breath.

I don't see this as much, but the guys tell me that Peck is really angry all the time, and that for some reason, he feels like he's not getting his due. He complains about people treating him like he's the low man on the totem pole. Problem is he never does anything to change that. He's disrespectful of my guys, guys with a lot of more experience than him. Borrows their tools, doesn't return them. Takes tools without asking, loses them. Never says he's sorry or replaces them. And when he's not going on about porn or some crazy racist conspiracy theories at lunch, he's grumbling about guys who he thinks don't deserve what they're getting. Basically, Peck is an asshole, and nobody likes him. My best's gonna quit if I ever hire him again.

I felt like I'd been punched in the gut.

Angel put his hand on my shoulder.

Should I stop?

I shook my head.

Lately, Peck's been complaining that he's getting the short end of the stick with condor duty. And he isn't wrong. Night shoots, he's pretty much always up in the air. Who wants to be the guy bunked down in a basket by himself night after night, peeing in a bottle and hauling his lunch up on a rope? No one. And he always is, but there's a reason. And that is, he wouldn't have a job otherwise. Why? Because, like I said, people don't want him around. One of the actors almost punched him. The DP has banned him from camera. Gaffer won't even let him bag a light stand or put on a rain hat, and my guys, well, my guys have had it up to here with his shitting on them.

The other night's a good example. We had this kid come in, new day-player, black kid, real young, not a lot of experience, half as much as Peck, but unlike Peck, he's a totally gung ho guy, willing to do anything—I mean anything—help anyone who asks, totally positive attitude, wardrobe, makeup, craft service. And he's also really a natural mechanical guy, knows cars, ropes. You know, a young Tony Jackson.

I nodded. I did recognize my mentor in the description.

So, there's no way I'm going to stick him in the bucket all night. He's too goddamned useful. So, then, when my best boy is telling everybody what they're gonna be doing, and he points at the condor for Peck, Peck loses it. Are you kidding? He's screaming, and this is close to camera, so everyone hears it. You're choosing that gangbanger over me? Fuck you! Fuck all of you! And he walks, throwing shit and pushing people out of his way.

I chewed on what Angel had told me for a few minutes and then pushed myself up off the curb. My knees wouldn't bend. I shook them until they popped.

Tell your guys I'll cover the costs of whatever he lost or broke.

You don't have to do that, Samson.

Sure, I do.

Angel nodded.

I'm sorry about all this.

I know you are Angel.

No hard feelings, I hope. I love your boy, you know, and that won't change.

I started to ask him if that were true—if anyone could actually love Peck. Instead, I said

No hard feelings.

He got up more easily than I had and hugged me.

Go home and get some sleep.

I hadn't known until he said it that sleep wasn't in the cards.

No rest for the weary, pal. I'm headed to my day job.

Angel smiled the smile of a man wondering if the color of the grass was different on my side of the fence. He threw his sandwich wrapper in a passing trash can.

What is it like being above-the-line?

Not everything it's cracked up to be. Shemahn's expecting an Oscar nomination.

Angel absorbed that without judgment.

How's that going?

Turns out getting her to the moon would be easier.

Is she helping?

Sure … in *her* way. She took me on a field trip to a Blacks Only meeting a few weeks ago.

Blacks Only? To get her an Oscar?

That's the idea.

He was skeptical.

And how'd they feel about having you drop in on them?

Like you'd expect. They don't call themselves Blacks Only for no reason. 'Course, they didn't really appreciate Shemahn confusing their movement with her career opportunity either. You could see them trying to figure out what to do with her—some way she could benefit the cause. And you know her, she's up for it.

Angel laughed at the description of our field trip.

Well, I hope screenwriting doesn't go sideways on you.

Me too.

He took one step toward his car and then turned back to me.

Peck's just a kid, Samson. He's gonna make mistakes. They all do. He'll snap out of this sooner or later.

I didn't share with him that that was what the Ex and I had been telling ourselves for years. I watched him get in his car and drive off then I texted Alex:

Sorry about my kid the other night.

I was on the freeway and starting to worry when I got his reply:

Hey, man, what you gonna do?

Tuesday, 8:45 a.m.

Alex and Angel were probably right. What could I do? Nothing, but show me a father who believes that. Show me a father who can actually do nothing when his kid's a fuckup like Atticus. I doubt that's you. I promise you: that's not me.

I didn't go straight to stretched out on Hildy's bed. I took a detour instead—straight up the 110 to the 101 and over the

Cahuenga Pass, wishing I had toothpicks for my eyelids as I shuffled along with every other worker bee zombie trapped in the morning rush hour.

I got to Atticus's house just before nine. I parked on the street and walked down the driveway toward the bungalow, smiling when I saw it because it always made me smile. In a lot of ways, it was a carbon copy of my place in Mar Vista— or what my place would be if I ever got it rebuilt. This bungalow was nestled in the back of a hidden garden full of ferns and gardenia and shaded by an enormous Tipawana; the bungalow might have started life as a pool house or a garage, but it was way more than that now. It was a fairly normal LA thing to do to turn your garage into a rental, but most of them were butt-ugly. Not this one. The owners had spent real money on it, and it had charm. It was a refuge from the nonstop bullshit storm of life in LA. Standing in that garden, you'd never have known there was an eight-lane freeway two blocks away.

I crossed the wide redwood deck to get to the pair of french doors that served as the entrance. I could see that the inside door was wide open. I put my face up to the screen.

Anyone home?

I batted the screen with my open palm, but that didn't really produce a sound that would get anyone's attention.

Atticus? Francesca?

Nothing.

Hey, it's me, Sam. Dad.

Still nothing.

What I did next wasn't the smartest thing to do in any town, but particularly in Los Angeles where people mostly don't ask people into their homes. I put my hand on the screen door handle and pulled. Maybe I could say I was surprised that the door wasn't locked, but I wasn't so surprised that I didn't step across the threshold like it was no big deal. That's when I heard the ratchet of a round being chambered in a shotgun.

That's far enough, Mr. Agonistes.

It was a man, obviously not my son, but clearly someone who knew me—or *of* me.

Sorry, sorry!

I put my hands up, retreated, and let the screen door flop closed.

I thought my son, Atticus, lived here.

Peck's gone.

Gone? Really? You a friend of his?

Not exactly.

A friend of Francesca's then?

Not exactly.

So, you two are hanging out?

Not exactly.

Is Francesca around?

Nope. I watch the place for her while she's at work.

Her place needs watching? Why?

Francesca hates violence.

What violence?

I looked around the garden and took in the utter peacefulness of the place. I couldn't believe any criminal would be able to find it let alone disrupt it. That was when I realized who Francesca was worried about. I wondered what the man holding the shotgun knew.

Do you know what she's scared of?

Not exactly.

How about approximately then?

Ask her yourself.

Okay, well, maybe you can remind me where she works then?

I hesitated.

I'm sorry … I don't know your name.

Better that way.

As you like. You're the one holding the gun.

Safety's on if that's what's freakin' you.

I think it's more of the entire situation, son.

I fell back on that reflexive generational diminutive and felt the tension it introduced immediately.

I ain't your son, Mr. Agonistes.

Sorry, old habits.

You better be going now.

You were going to tell me where I could find Francesca.

Not exactly. I'll tell her you were looking for her. Up to her what she has to do with you and yours.

Would you mind if I came inside and left her a note?

I would. Like father, like son—if you know what I mean.

No, I don't.

Your son's an entitled fuckin' douche.

Mr. Not Exactly suddenly had a lot to say.

Even though his name ain't on the lease—even though this was Francesca's place since before Peck came along—he acted like she didn't have the right to kick him out. She tried to be nice, but he just slapped her around. She didn't want to call the cops, so she called me. Took me and a bunch of my friends to convince him.

The anger from him caught me off guard, but not so much that I validated it.

Well, it must be sweet for you now, taking advantage of Francesca when she's so vulnerable.

Not exactly.

Mr. Not Exactly was back. I knew he had recognized the insult, but it didn't irritate him.

Francesca ain't over him. Hard to figure.

I couldn't—

Hey, fuck off now. I'm tired of talking to you. You're almost as bad as your son for wearing out a welcome.

⋛⋋⋛⋋⋛⋋⋛⋋⋛

I called my Ex from the car.

Where's Francesca work?

Why?

I need to talk to her.

I already left her a message. Let's just wait. She'll call back.

Maybe.

Why do you say that?

I went by Atticus's on my way home.

That's not on the way from Long Beach to Mar Vista.

What difference does it make? I was in the car already.

And?

Sounds like Francesca wanted him out of her place. And he made a mess of it. There was some asshole with a shotgun standing guard in case Atticus comes back. Told me Atticus was an entitled douche. Trotted out that old like father, like son crap. Can you believe it?

I don't know how we got here, Sam

She said.

Which was not exactly comforting from my paternal point of view. I took some deep breaths.

What did Angel say?

About what?

Don't be cute, Sam.

I went for long story short.

It's worse than we thought. Atticus has a 'people' problem. Basically, he's an asshole to everyone, but particularly to people who work hard and get ahead. And his racist tendencies are still trending.

Fuck.

Yup. So, where's she work then?

She'll call back.

Before or after that kid blows our son's head off?

That was enough to convince her.

On Ventura. In Encino. Same building as our last marriage counselor. You'll recognize it when you see it. I don't remember the name of the dentist she works for, but it's on the fifth floor.

Same building as Dr. Hansel, eh?

Yes. That'll give you a little trip down memory lane. What are you going to say to Francesca?

I'm going to ask her what constitutes a douche in this day and age.

Sam, you don't really think she's right, do you?

What difference does it make what an old fuck like me thinks? Francesca and Angel and that asshole with the shotgun have the mic now.

And Petunia Biggars, I thought, if she's still alive.

What if she won't answer you?

I don't know. Drop in on dear old Dr. Hansel for some parenting postmortem. Confess my failures, my manly shortcomings. Talk about what a bad example I was. Like father, like son etcetera.

Sam, your real problem is that you haven't had enough sleep to talk to anyone, let alone your son's ex-girlfriend. It's not going to help if she—

I hung up before she could finish telling me what to do.

Tuesday, 11:00 a.m.

I should have let her finish.

I mean, in spite of our not having lived under the same roof for more than ten years, my Ex still knew me pretty well. Running on fumes was never my strong suit—even when I was younger and rolling from one feature to the next. Most crew people got used to being sleep-deprived by the end of a shoot. Not me. Working lots of overtime—eighteen- or twenty-hour days like we sometimes had to near the end of a picture—always flattened me. Worse than losing my hair even. She was right. I should have gone straight home to bed rather than heading west to talk to Francesca. Probably should have waited for her to call my Ex back, but I told myself she was on my way home, which was mostly true.

Don't get me wrong. It wasn't a disaster. Not in my opinion.

Although I did fall asleep waiting for her.

How is that not a disaster exactly?

Well, as soon as I opened the door of the dentist's office and saw that waiting room full of kids and their parents, I changed my mind about talking to Francesca at work. She wouldn't be comfortable or forthcoming, and I would end up getting frustrated and shown the door. I remembered the little café in the lobby next to the elevators and figured, in the way only a sleep-deprived person can figure, that sooner or later, Francesca would have to take a coffee break or a lunch break and would go down to the café.

I got myself a five-dollar cup of bad coffee, a *Variety*, and some French-like breakfast pastries and set myself up at a table where I could see the elevators in the lobby. I spread open the magazine and pretended to be enjoying a leisurely morning. Why it didn't occur to me that she might have brought her own lunch or be working a short shift and take the elevator straight to the garage when she was done, I don't know.

I propped my head up on my right hand, fought the Sandman until I passed out, and slept until someone kicked my chair leg. Due to which, my elbow slipped on the magazine, my chin cracked the table edge, and my head rung like a church bell.

It was the owner of the café.

No homeless sleeping here. Find a shelter.

I blinked up at a very well-groomed guy about my age wearing what looked like a traditional East Indian suit. I couldn't place the accent. Indian? Indonesian? Pakistani? My mind toggled between wondering why he thought I was homeless and how he had such a handsome head of hair.

Out! Out! Out!

He shouted.

No *please*. No respect for the customer. I tried to get up, but I couldn't find my balance. It didn't help that he was kicking my chair. It never occurred to me to protest, to wave him away, to ask how long a paying customer was allowed to sit at a table in his café. It was only when I realized that I might have missed Francesca that my mind cleared enough to form words.

What time is it?

No matter, no matter. Your time is up!

He was trying to pull the chair out from under me.

Up? There's a time limit?

Certainly, certainly.

I could feel my blood rising. My fists were clinched. It might have turned ugly, but then I heard a woman say,

It's all right, Saeed. I know him.

And there was Francesca smiling at me across the small café table.

All right, my dear, but you must take this filthy man with you when you are finished.

Of course.

She smiled sweetly at the café owner, but she was bubbling at me, every sentence rising to a combination question/exclamation point.

Hello, Mr. A! What a nice surprise to see you! What a coincidence! Are you here for an appointment with a doctor? Did you know I worked here?

It occurred to me that Francesca was a genuinely nice, unsuspecting person—and that my son had made a big mistake by screwing things up with her.

It's not a coincidence, Francesca. I came here hoping to talk to you.

Even knowing I wanted to talk to her did not dampen her enthusiasm.

Really? What about?

Atticus.

She was still smiling, but the light in her eyes did dim. She was wary. On edge even. I was happy that she was tougher than she appeared.

We're not together anymore, Mr. A.

No more happy questioning lilt.

Yes, I know that.

I don't really want to talk about the past.

She looked at her watch.

And I have a patient in ten minutes. I just came down for a cup of coffee.

I was hoping you could tell me what happened to him.

She reddened. She looked at her hands. She started to speak and then stopped herself. She tried again.

Look, Peck and I broke up. That's all I have to say about it. More than that, you'll have to ask him.

I will. If I can find him.

What do you mean?

He lost his shit and walked off set Friday night. Nobody's seen or heard from him since.

She considered this.

I haven't spoken to him if that's what you're wondering.

It's not.

What are you asking me then?

I guess I want to understand why he's so angry. I mean, things seemed to be going so much better for him, and I know he really liked you.

Francesca glazed over. She gave no indication one way or the other if she believed that.

How about telling me why the guy guarding your place called him a douche?

She swallowed hard but remained silent.

I know he's had his moments, but I don't remember Atticus treating you badly. Did he?

She crossed her arms across her chest.

I don't want to be hurtful, but I don't think you have any idea what kind of son you raised. Somewhere along the way, he got the wrong idea about how to treat people, women in particular.

What's that mean?

He's not considerate. He acts like the golden rule doesn't apply to him.

Okay. Is there something specific?

These things are between Peck and me, Mr. A. I don't want to talk to you about them.

Can't you tell me anything?

She weighed a response. She pursed her lips. It looked like she was barely holding back tears.

As long as I've known him, Peck has spent most of his free time on the internet. I did not know or care what he was looking at. Then, not too long ago, a friend of mine showed me the hateful things he says in chat rooms. Peck blames immigrants and minorities for all the problems in this country. He makes up stories about people like my parents to cause them trouble. He threatens women for fun. When he's frustrated, he hits things. He's full of hate.

Christ! I hope he never hit you.

This broke the dam. She put both hands over her face and wept silently.

I'm sorry.

She pushed her chair back from the table without uncovering her face. She was getting up to leave.

This homeless guy making you cry, Francesca?

Saeed was back again.

Shall I kick him to the curb for you?

I jumped up.

What's your problem, pal? No one kicks people to the curb in America. And I'm not homeless—so stop saying that.

No fuckin' way, man. You're homeless. I can smell it all over you.

He sniffed me.

I took a deep breath and tried to lower my blood pressure. When that didn't work, I lowered my voice instead.

Why are you harassing me? All I did was come and spend my money in your overpriced cafe.

I harass you because I like to harass you. I say you're homeless because I like to say you're homeless. Freedom of speech, right? First Amendment, right? Go back to your tent in the bushes, you useless old white man!

I really couldn't figure out why this guy seemed to hate me so much. The fumes I had in the tank couldn't handle a fight with him, but I did want an answer to one question.

Where do you fuckin'—

Francesca stopped crying and pulled me out of the coffee shop and into the elevator lobby.

You need to go before you cause any more trouble, Mr. A.

She was rubbing away her tears with the heels of her hands.

Me? I couldn't believe the injustice of what had just happened, but I bit my tongue.

I'm really sorry. I'm sorry that my son turned into such a shit.

Peck has always been a shit, Mr. A. He didn't turn into one. I guess it's my own fault for thinking I could change him. I thought that if I loved him enough, he would want to change, that he would turn out to be a keeper, but I was wrong. You didn't raise a keeper.

He's only twenty-five years old. We can't just cut him loose. Don't we have to try to help him?

Francesca might have been genuinely nice at any other time, but this time, she did not pull any punches.

I don't know much about you, Mr. A, but if you ask me, I think you missed your chance a long time ago. Peck is too far gone.

She got on the elevator and stared at me from the ground zero of her disappointment as the doors closed.

I walked across the lobby as Saeed blocked the open door of his café, arms crossed with the certainty of his judgment, quietly singing without any of Paul Simon's sweetness or moonlight.

Homeless … homeless …

Tuesday, 12:30 p.m.

When I got back to Mar Vista, two guys in dark suits appeared out of nowhere and followed me up the walk to my front door.

Look, fellas

I said —whatever they were selling, I wasn't in the buying mood—

I've been up all night, and I really can't waste my time on a Latter-day double-team.

Sam Agonistes?

Some wonky synapse fired in my brain and came up with a new explanation.

Oh

I said

Not Mormons, you're the exterminators. I never heard back on when you'd be coming. Tell your dispatcher he's lucky I was home.

Exterminators?

One of them, I couldn't say which, spoke, but they both look confused.

Exterminators, wranglers, animal control, call yourself whatever you have to so the tree huggers will leave you in peace. I just need someone to get rid of this goddamn raccoon. I've had it up to here with all those softhearted do-nothings spouting their 'this was their yard before it was your yard' nonsense. A wild animal does not get a yard—at least not in Mar Vista. I'm happy to live and let live as long as my way of life isn't what's lost. Besides, we know the raccoons are just fucking with us for their own goddamned amusement. Poison, traps, dart guns, I don't care what you use. You should park your truck around back.

They looked at me like I was crazy. And when I think back on it, maybe I was.

It's an SUV.

They turned and pointed at their heavily tinted black Suburban.

This is a goddamned vicious monster raccoon, at least half my size. You'll need a truck with a cage.

We're not exterminators, Mr. Agonistes. We're here on official business.

Official business? Really? In that case let's skip back to the part about not wasting my time.

Is your nation's security a waste of time, Mr. Agonistes?

I had a hard time not cracking up at the ersatz *Dragnet* of their performance, but it did help me concentrate on who they actually were: two young white guys, practically clones of one another and almost too photogenic to be allowed out in public. Hard to believe you could find two people so identical as these two though: same height and weight, muscled-up, crew cuts. You know the way Hollywood casts heavies these days. It's like they're warning us the people we really have to fear are the supermodels.

I'm guessing you want me to say no.

Look, Agonistes, we'd like to play nice.

Almost in unison, they both pulled back their suit jackets to reveal the Glocks holstered on their hips.

But one way or the other you're gonna give us what we came for.

I am?

I said even as the thought bubble over my head went: Are you kidding me? Who wrote this dialogue? This is worse than anything I wrote on my worst day.

Then I realized that this wasn't scripted. These guys hadn't been cast in these parts; they were just extras tossing lines out in the hopes of being noticed. These clowns were just refugee extras from *Men in Black,* angling for an upgrade.

You guys could use few more rehearsals. Plus work on the timing for the Glocks reveal.

They flinched but ignored my direction.

Be nicer inside.

Could get hot out here.

New thought bubble: What is it with strangers trying to get into my house all the time?

I looked around my neighborhood. Nothing new. Another red flag day: deserted, dusty streets, hot wind, nobody out in their yards. Déjà vu all over again.

This is LA. It's hot no matter where you are

I said.

Neither of them liked this, but I didn't care. One of them, the one who I identified by his cleft chin, produced an envelope, pulled out some headshots, and tried to hand them to me. He shook them to indicate that I was supposed to take them, but I didn't.

This isn't casting

I said, glancing back at my bungalow for inspiration

This is story. Casting's moved off the lot. Too many wannabe actors wandering around loose.

He ignored my wisecrack.

Recognize her?

Sure I did but I didn't say that. The image was blurry, but she was unmistakable: it was Petunia Biggars. It didn't take a rocket scientist to realize that official business or bullshit this was the danger she was afraid of. They might not be the first team, but they were armed.

I shook my head.

You sure? Take a closer look. Hey, you want 'em, you can have 'em. We have a lot more.

No-Cleft was trying to keep it light, no big deal.

I made a show of leaning closer, then leaning back, I shook my head again.

You are *the* Sam Agonistes, the retired key grip turned screenwriter, who's rumored to have saved the life of the pop star Shemahn?

That is the rumor.

Sometimes called Samson?

You seem to know a lot about me.

That's our job, isn't it?

Hey

I said

I know a lot about me too. Probably more than the two of you combined. You think maybe your employer would be interested in hiring me to replace you? Cut his payroll in half.

Don't be stupid. That's not our only job. What we really do is help people who need help.

Does the lady in this picture need your help?

She's confused. We're good at clearing up confusion.

Something inside me, a known unknown that had been holding its breath, relaxed. The bad guys were still looking for Petunia. She had gotten away.

Confused describes a lot of people these days. It's a public service what you're doing.

I commiserated with them. They were bewildered. My gut instinct was to double down, so I tickled them with a real wild hair.

Hey, since you guys want to help, not exterminate, maybe you could help me and my Ex. We need to find our son,

Atticus. He's the definition of not thinking clearly. Trust me, he—we—I could sure use your help.

I was irritating them, but I didn't care. The more I talked, the clearer it became to me that they should be looking for Atticus, not Petunia. And once I started into Atticus's troubles, I couldn't stop myself.

He flamed out at his job. His girlfriend threw him out for being a douche. There's a guy with a shotgun waiting to put some slugs in his ass. He's not answering his phone. Nobody's seen him since Friday night. You can see I got a real missing person case on my hands. His mom's pulling her hair out. I would be too if I had any to pull. We could go to the cops, but they're only going to give us the old ain't-a minor-ain't-been-gone-long-enough runaround. I've tried looking for him myself, but I don't really have the tools in my toolbox you guys do—mirrored shades, tinted windows, jailhouse songbirds—you know, all your official stuff for tracking someone down. I'm sorry I can't help you find this young lady, but maybe you could nose around for Atticus instead. It'd really be a help.

Without blinking, they broke rule number one of improv: they didn't say yes.

Look, Mr. Agonistes. Now you're wasting everybody's time. We have information that the woman in the picture came to see you yesterday.

What, like surveillance footage or something? Is there a drone up there following me?

I put my hand up to my eyes to scout the skies.

Fuck this. Show him the other pics

Cleft said.

The other pics were shot on the same long lens, same blurriness, but this time, they were photos of me and Shemahn and Shemahn's assistant, Ja'K, at the Blacks Only meeting. In one of the photos, Petunia was standing just behind an out-of-focus white person. His face wasn't necessarily mine, but I knew it was. Still, I shook my head.

What do you mean no?

Picture two cartoon versions of people blowing their tops.

That's you, isn't it? That's your producing partner, Shemahn. And that's the girl we were asking you about in the background.

You didn't ask about me or Shemahn. And I'm not saying that is or isn't me. Could be. I just don't recognize that woman you're trying to *help*.

I did the air quotes thing.

You know it's a crime to lie to an agent of the government?

Is that what you two monkeys are? Authorized blah-blah secret agents? Not extras shouting out lines hoping the ADs will have to upgrade you to day-player on set?

I don't know what it was about them that made me push back so aggressively. Maybe the fact that they had flashed Glocks instead of their identification. Maybe because the way they were acting told me that even if they were FBI or NSA or DOJ, they were doing something they didn't want anyone to know they were doing. Maybe it was because I was still Samson and didn't knuckle under for made-up truths and unvarnished bullshit.

You have something with your pictures that says—hey, hey, hello my name is Clarice, and I work for the Federal Bureau of Helping Out Confused Fuckers? No? Why are you shaking your heads no?

They kept their tempers but confirmed my suspicion.

We have reason to believe that this young woman took refuge in your home.

Whoever she is, she'd be very surprised to hear that.

If she's not in there, you shouldn't have a problem with us seeing for ourselves.

Sorry, I didn't have time to drywall before I went to work.

You may be charged with harboring a fugitive who fled federal custody in the possession of items vital to the national security of your country.

Would that go on my permanent record?

They mistook this sarcasm as me finally seeing the error of my ways.

Definitely, but not if we can tell the judge you cooperated.

They made as if to go past me into the house.

You're way off script here, fellas. You'd have to have a warrant to get inside my house.

It was clear that they did not. Cleft puffed himself up like he was about to take a run at me, but his partner held him back.

No-Cleft played good cop.

I think we've gotten off on the wrong foot here, Samson. I know it may have sounded like it, but we're not really threatening you.

He took off his sunglasses and smiled. His eyes were steely blue; I couldn't help thinking that he should forget acting and focus on his supermodeling, and I almost said so.

I mean, I'm sure the three of us are on the same side here. We all just want what's best for the good old U S of A, right? We have a good life in this country. The best on earth. We don't want a bunch of ingrates upsetting the apple cart just because they don't have apples where they come from.

I resisted the temptation to say I hated apples.

And I can appreciate what happened to you. This very forward black woman talks her way into your home, comes on to you as women like her are wont to, and you're a man, you may be retired, but you're clearly still very fit, so you do what any of us would do: succumb to your animal instincts. And now you're embarrassed. It's already been tough explaining why you need to work for one of them.

The fumes inside me exploded.

Get the fuck off my property!

They didn't move.

You're making a big mistake, Sam.

I said get the fuck off my property!

No-Cleft tossed the pictures toward me; they bounced off my dunlap and fluttered down around my feet.

That's a Blacks Only meeting you were at. Bad things have happened to those people. Just because you're white, don't think bad things can't happen to you too.

Then Cleft and No-Cleft turned in unison and stalked back to their SUV. I stood my ground until they slammed their doors and locked themselves in. Then I stumbled back into my house. In spite of their warning, I wasn't thinking about anything: not the fact that the Upgrades were clearly staking me out, not my douche son, not Blacks Only, or whether or not Petunia Biggars was right about my being simultaneously up to my neck and full of shit. I didn't have enough left in the tank for anything but crawling into bed and watching the last of my fumes aurora borealis from my eyeballs.

Tuesday, 4:00-ish p.m.

Is that what a gripster wears?

What?

Someone was talking to me in my sleep again, but I didn't care, I wanted to know what a "gripster" was.

Was this what you were wearing when you saved her life?

I heard the sound of a long fingernail scraping stiff cotton, and then the image of a juvenile raccoon hanging off the bib of my overalls jolted me to consciousness. It wasn't a raccoon. It was Ja'K, Shemahn's personal assistant, scratching at my pant leg. I sat up and kicked my feet to the floor. It didn't feel like I'd been asleep long enough to get up, but I didn't like the idea of being flat on my back with him so close to me.

How did he get in? Did I forget to set the alarm?

It won't be boffo box office if the man who saves her dresses like a cracker

Ja'K had more costume tips.

I looked at what I was wearing—Carhartt overalls, a MD3 T-shirt, and a fleece jacket from *Whiter Shade of*

Pale—my regular grip clothes for night exteriors—and tried to remember if this was what I was wearing on the night in question. It seemed likely.

What's a gripster?

You Samson, you're a gripster. Is that your password?

I focused. Ja'K was holding my laptop.

What?

Your password. I need your password so I can read the script. You have a deadline, remember? Shemahn sent me here to make sure you don't blow it. I tried my name, my name spelled backwards, my name all caps.

Why the fuck would your name be my password?

I stood up and grabbed the computer from him. On my feet, I had nearly a foot on the kid, plus probably a hundred pounds. There wasn't much to him: mind or body.

I'm not telling you my password—and you're not reading my screenplay till I say you can.

Ja'K was so full of himself he wasn't offended.

Maybe we should make it a Google Doc so I can comment in real time. Remember what we decided about your deadline.

Fuck your bullshit deadline!

I lost it.

With one word, Ja'K suckered me right up to edge of self-destruction before I stopped and found my balance again. I glared down at him like an angry bear; he blinked up at me like a Disney bunny. I could've squashed him but he wasn't worth it. I just couldn't allow myself to forget that.

Ja'K hadn't been around when I first worked with Shemahn. There had been another assistant, Lilah, a girl from her hometown, a sharper tool than Ja'K, but for some reason, she'd gotten the boot. Shemahn had introduced her new assistant at a development meeting a few months back, and before you could count to ten, it was *All About Eve*, sort of. Even though as far as I could tell, he was some wet-behind-the-ears kid with no education and no resume. He was full of opinions from the get-go; sadly, nobody including me, had had the balls to tell him to fuck off. Mostly because Shemahn gave him the conch and never took it back. The way I figured it, I didn't need to worry since I outranked all of them. As long as my connection to Shemahn stayed strong, it wouldn't matter who came and went. Kids like Ja'K were always short-timers. He would eventually wear Shemahn out, telling her all the time what she could or couldn't do; the guy who saved her life would still be standing when he was out the door. Until then, I would just have to put up with his tricks.

Like this bullshit deadline which came out of the blue thirty-six hours ago on High Noon Monday.

He called in the middle of breakfast to inform me that they, meaning he and Shemahn, but really him, were giving me a deadline.

Deadlines are good. Americans need deadlines

He said.

Why's that?

I said, slurping my coffee close to the phone to annoy him.

To be our best.

What if my best doesn't do deadlines?

Don't be like that, Samson.

Name's Sam.

He skipped past my objection, ignored my slurping.

We need pages by Saturday.

Why so long?

I asked.

Why not make it tomorrow? Or better yet, yesterday? And as long as we're handing out deadlines, what's yours?

He hung up without saying.

Don't get me wrong. I've always been good under pressure. Never cracking's how I made it to the top of grip-dom. I'm at my best when the AD's screaming about losing the light or running out of time on some five-year-old kid, but that's real pressure; those are real deadlines. I love them. I'm just not a guy who responds well to bullshit. Made-up bullshit dreamed up by a little shit who doesn't know shit. That's Hollywood. Making up crap so he can puff himself up with it and pretend he's more than an assistant.

To my point about deadlines, in the day and a half since Ja'K called, I haven't put a word on the page. I haven't even thought of a word besides "fuck you." Okay, that's two words, but you get the point. Not that it matters what he says or I do. 'Cause everyone knows who the boss is. Most of all, me. That's why I didn't go over his head and call Shemahn to protest the bullshit. I try never to bother her with the nonsense. It's a waste of her time. Plus, she's too classy for this shit.

I'll give you an example. On the first day on the first picture I did with her—back in my key grip days—we were shooting a scene in the backyard of the house where her character lived. She'd just flown in that morning from New York. She'd had a concert the night before. The AD warned us all to be on our best behavior since she didn't know us and hadn't slept. In other words, don't fuck with her, which was easy since she didn't make a big deal of anything. There was no fuss. No whining. She went right into makeup and then came to straight to the set. In between setups she didn't run to her trailer, she just napped in a hammock in a neighbor's yard. She'd gone up to the neighbor's door herself and asked if they would mind her using their hammock. Big surprise, they didn't. So, this is to say, with Shemahn, I know who I'm dealing with: a supertalented, genuinely nice person.

What I don't know is how a chart-topping, sweet, twentysomething pop star with a massive preteen following and a couple of supporting roles in features—one as the girlfriend of a car thief and the other as the daughter of an embezzler—finds the chops to carry a serious dramatic picture all the way to critical acclaim. Shemahn wants to expand her audience, grow her demographic. She thinks a star vehicle that will reset all the preconceived notions about her will do that. Not that I blame her for wanting out of her bubblegummed-up pigeonhole. And who am I to doubt her, seeing as she didn't doubt me? Maybe she has the chops. She's clearly talented. Extra. Why shouldn't she have a chance to prove herself? I'm just grateful for the opportunity to be her opportunity. 'Course trusting anyone with your future in this town can turn out to be big mistake.

Like this kid Ja'K, trying to break into my computer while I'm sleeping. My trust would be the last thing I'd give a known unknown like him.

Where in the valley are you from, Ja'K?

Is that a clue? Is Arvin your password? I know, It's Weed Patch!

You just don't seem like you're from LA.

I'm not. I'm French Algerian, but I've lived in California all my life.

And your name, Ja'K? Is that French or Algerian?

It's Hollywood. Jack without a C. My birth certificate says Jacques Kiscur, but I wanted to fit in, so I changed it to Jack. Then when I was in seventh grade, there were four Jacks in my class, so they called me Jack K. Now I'm in show biz, and I've just taken some creative license.

How did you end up working for Shemahn?

Miss Mahn and I met at a Grammy's after-party. Kismet, right?

Kismet for Kiscur, I thought. That was inevitable.

Okay.

I pushed past him to go to the kitchen. I was suddenly very thirsty.

So, why do you think you can invade my home without me standing my ground and shooting you?

You weren't at the office.

That's not an answer.

You really shouldn't be sleeping on my dime. You're supposed to be writing my screenplay.

Your dime? *Your* screenplay? First of all, there aren't any dimes because there's no production deal. And second of all, this will be *my* screenplay for Shemahn to star in. My screenplay *does not* belong to anyone but me, Ja'K.

Don't worry. I'm sure we can fix that problem.

He was infuriating.

What do you want?

He switched to excitement at the least concession.

Well, Miss Mahn and I really had the creative juices flowing this a.m. when we came up with something that we both think could really knock it out of the ballpark, so she sent me over posthaste to stop you and whatever you were doing so you could write a home run instead.

I let out a loud raspberry, acting more irritated than I really was. I would accept help from the trash if it would get me unstuck.

Stop fuckin' around. I'm pretty far along with the Blacks Only angle.

Well, I'm sorry about that, but this is a grand slam, a high-concept no-brainer. And most of all, Miss Mahn really likes this idea a lot. This is the film with the heart and the depth that will get her a star on the Walk of Fame.

She already has a star.

He didn't care. He was pitching. Mark my words. This is the film that will get our names above the title. Of course, if you can find a way to keep what you've done—work it into our no-brainer—great, but otherwise, you'll just have to round file it, as they say.

I growled to keep up the pretense.

It's not really up to you, is it, Samson?

You are not allowed to call me that!

I snapped, but then I decided my name wasn't worth a showdown with a punk kid. Shemahn and I were co-presidents of our company. That's what mattered. Whatever film we made would be a Samson Production, plain and simple. Ja'K would get a credit, but it wouldn't be above the title or even in the mains if I had anything to say about it.

Okay, let's hear it.

He took a deep breath.

Fade in.

He made air quotes as he said the words and then stopped.

That's how films start, right?

Why not?

He rewound.

Fade in.

More air quotes and big arm waving to suggest clearing away a fog.

Camera swoops down on an awkward adolescent, in some socially unsafe place, like a high school homecoming dance or gym class or some ilk, you decide, and the camera senses a cesspool of hostility, a confusion of sexuality and gender, wondering who they are, how they will ever survive in a hostile world.

Ja'K's rendition was more like a narrated interpretive dance around my kitchen than a story pitch. I didn't like to admit it, but it—he—was charming. Almost innocent. I didn't bother taking notes.

Then somehow, fill the somehow in later, they discover that their gender is not innate but born of the cesspool. They feel trapped inside the sex that society has assigned them. They don't know if they want to transition completely, but they do want to explore the fluidity that they—

So, how many characters exactly are experiencing hostility and confusion at this point?

One.

They is one?

I said even though I already knew the answer.

Yes. They are so ahead of their time that they have rejected the gender binary, defied convention, and freed themselves from all societal constructs.

I could only sigh. I felt the thumbscrews of social evolution tighten. Okay. They is one. Go on.

So, we also see that they have music in their soul. They are a vital creative force for good in the Universe with a capital U. We see them express themselves and are enthralled. Swept into a world of emotional sunshine.

By what exactly?

We'll fill that in later. What does it matter really? They are so talented their genius cannot be understood. What matters is that they are pushing against the oppression of hundreds of years of society's conception of them, the slavery of body and the chains of the male gaze. And then one day, something happens, what exactly we'll have to fill that in later, but they have an epiphany and they act, bravely breaking the chains of sex, braving the dreaded knife to exchange penis for vagina, to bring breasts from nothing—

Hold it. Hold it!

Ja'K finished a slow twirl, tilted his head to the side, and gazed at me with a kind postorgasmic euphoria.

Let me get this straight: Shemahn is going to play the part of a boy who decides he wants to be a girl and then has a sex change operation?

No, Samson

He purred. Ja'K was too euphoric to be angry.

You can't have a person who identifies as a woman in gender, sexuality, and sex play a transgendered, transsexual youth. That would be immoral.

Like Mickey Rooney in *Breakfast at Tiffany's*?

Mickey who?

Or Johnny Depp in *The Lone Ranger*?

Sounds like history to me. This is reality, Samson.

So, 'they' will be played by someone else. Not Shemahn. What's her part?

TBD.

Shemahn's okay with her Oscar winning part being TBD?

We didn't bother with trivial details. Trivia stifles the creative flow.

I decided not to mention to Ja'K that Shemahn's part wasn't really a trivial detail when it came to getting the picture financed. He was turning slow, blissed-out revolutions.

Here's an inspiration I had on my way over here: our protagonist is a genius musician, like Kanye, but they don't understand their talent. It's only when they are inspired by the touch of a beautiful pop star that they blow their own mind with creativity. Miss Mahn could play the inspirational pop star who discovers them in the crowd. Kismet, right?

What happens after the touch of the beautiful pop star?

We'll fill that in later.

That's a lot to fill in.

We can't do all your work for you.

More dreamy turns.

And do you have someone in mind for the transgendered, transsexual youth?

He closed his eyes.

We'd do a nationwide talent search, make a publicity stunt of it, find a diamond in the rough. A natural actor who is ethically pure and beautiful.

I still don't buy it. Shemahn said she would be okay with a supporting part?

Like I said, we didn't get to it, but Miss Mahn knows it's TBD. Making her a pop star's just my latest shot of brilliance. She hasn't heard it. She and I didn't want to waste a single minute before dictating it to you.

Maybe I should have left well enough alone since there was no way we were going to make this movie if Shemahn only had a cameo, but frankly, I was too much of an asshole when it came to Hollywood wannabes not to express myself now and then.

Listen, son, before I dive into a total rebuild of my script, I want to make sure my producing partner has signed off on only having a bit part in the movie that's supposed to reinvent her career. I need her to tell me that she doesn't have any issues with what is basically a C-A-M-E-O. Because actors don't usually win awards for cameos. So, before I head down this dead-end street, she needs to tell me she's okay with barely being in her movie.

Fuck, Samson, do you want this gig or not? Shemahn loves this idea, and it's your job to make sure she gets what she wants—everything she wants.

For all his charm and innocence, Ja'K didn't scare easy.

Everything?

Everything!

Last I heard, she wanted her character to be one of the founders of Blacks Only; she wanted to be able to demonstrate the range of an actor whose character lost her brother in a police shooting and then faces her fears of society's oppression to lead Blacks Only to national prominence.

Yeah, that's right.

Okay …

I drew the word out so that it was clear I thought this didn't add up with what he'd just dictated.

These things—*they*, the beautiful pop star, police shootings, and Blacks Only—do not belong in the same movie.

Look, do I have to do all the creating? You're the writer here. I'm just a producer.

Another know-nothing assistant turned producer. Before I knew it, he'd be the director, but I was still co-president ... for now.

Okay. Well ... how's this?

I pitched the first piece of nonsense that came into my head. Turns out my nonwriter's writer's block didn't stop me when it came to nonstarters.

So, we have this transgender youth who transitions and then she/they are killed by a homophobic white cop in the first act—but not before giving a hit song to the character played by Shemahn who goes on to found the Blacks Only in his/her/their honor in the second act.

The genius youth dies and is out of the picture?

He didn't like this—so I went all in on crazy.

Of course not, you didn't let me finish. They die, but then they don't go away. Kind of *Ghost and Mrs. Muir.*

No way, no ghosts. I don't like scary movies.

It's not scary, it's a classic. Check it out. The genius youth haunts Shemahn's character in the second act, trying to help her see that music is the only way to overcome the oppression of the white society, becoming her muse, inspiring the songs she sings and her transformation of society. So that in the end, Blacks Only marches to her music. And then when Shemahn makes peace with the 'man,' putting aside the fact that this woman you refer to as Miss Mahn will be making peace with the man is weird on the face of it ...

Air quotes with a vengeance ...

They do it by singing a duet of the martyred genius's song.

Ja'K flushed like he had raging fever.

Okay, okay, okay. Write that.

And that's what he actually expected me to do: open my laptop and write some out-of-my-ass, transgendered update of *The Ghost and Mrs. Muir*. And I have to admit I briefly considered trying to write that movie, but as I stood at my front door, watching him float to his car through the hot, flat light of an ominous afternoon and felt the resistance of the airless negative in my house with all the windows and curtains closed, I knew I couldn't. And it wasn't the fact that every day seemed hotter and dryer than the last, that we were living with endless red flag warnings, or that my house was a disaster; it was that I might be able to pitch nonsense, but I had enough self-respect not to believe in it.

The Upgrades were watching me from the front seat of their Suburban. I wondered what they thought they would learn by staking me out. I resisted the temptation to flip them off. I waved instead and went back inside. I made sure to lock both locks and put on the chain.

I heard my phone vibrate on the dining room table. I didn't have to look at the screen to know it was my Ex. She would have to wait. I needed more than a couple hours of sleep to talk to her. And there was no chance of her sneaking up on me again with the chain on the door. Thinking of her did, however, remind me that I had bottle of Herradura in the bar; a couple of shots of tequila would help with the heat. I slammed down four shots to be on the safe side, put the table fan on high, and wedged it between my legs so that it blew straight at my damp junk.

Wednesday, 3:30 a.m.

Once again, waking up was rough. Not because of the heat or the tequila and not because I hadn't slept enough. Without looking at the clock, I knew from the way the night air felt—heat giving up a few degrees—that it was after midnight. Ja'K had left before five, which meant I'd had ten hours. Even after a night exterior, that should be plenty.

You're probably wondering what's the deal with this guy? Can't he ever just get a restful eight hours? I don't have the answer to that one. Maybe it's me—or maybe it was just the kind of week I was having.

Anyway, what was really rough about this wake-up in a chain of rough ones was the feeling that there was something I was supposed to pay attention to. And I'm not talking about beating the made-up deadline or pulling Atticus back from the brink. Those things I didn't need reminding about.

This was a nagging something that started in a dream or a half dream/half stupor where I thought that there was someone at the door I was supposed to let in—only I couldn't conceive of what door and then I could barely hear the sound even though that's what wakes me up, until there's not even that, just the memory of it.

Raccoon, you're thinking. Obviously, but this wasn't a "wild monster coming for you" roar. This was more a "let me get what I came for in peace" shuffle. So, I waited for it to reveal its nature and wondered if I had dreamed it up.

After a bit, I sat up and turned off the fan. Immediately, there was a new, barely audible something, not roar or shuffle, but the sound of a body being dragged, dragging itself through the dirt. I hoped, in my heart and in my throat, that it was not Petunia, bloody and dying, using the last of her strength to get in my house. Then the dragging stopped too.

I stood up on the bed and put my ear to the wall. Nothing. I pulled back the blind and looked out into the yard. There was no moon, and my motion detector lights weren't triggered, so I couldn't see squat. Still, I calmed down enough to explore a little. As a precaution against giving myself away, I crawled from room to room, peeking through the curtains and under the blinds.

You could say it was pointless to crawl around a dark house in the middle of the night. No one could see me. And you'd be right, except for the way I was thinking. It was more along the lines of—if a man is alone in the forest, and there's no woman to hear him, is he still wrong? And this was my forest. And I couldn't afford to be wrong.

On all fours, I didn't see anything that explained what I'd heard. The stakeout continued. The SUV hadn't moved, but I couldn't see right away if the Upgrades were actually in the car. It didn't take much to suspect them. And at first, when I couldn't see people, I was sure it had been them rustling in the bushes and spying on me.

The light of a cell phone screen illuminated a face, and then the one in the driver's seat lit a cigarette. They didn't seem to have moved since I waved at them. What I heard could've been the Santa Anas coming up or one of the neighbors getting home late. A few second-floor windows were glowing with the blue light of television screens. Neighbors could be the explanation. Or maybe I had dreamed all of it. Maybe it was just a guilty conscience inventing the sound of Petunia coming back.

I got up and walked back toward the kitchen, but I left the lights off. Even though I was hungry, I didn't open the refrigerator. I didn't want anything to signal to those monkeys outside what I was up to. I found some saltines and peanut butter, sat at the dining room table, made little sandwiches, and thought about what was next. Writing was out of the question—and so was searching the internet for info on Atticus. I didn't want my laptop to give me away. I could have gone back to bed, but I wasn't tired.

I was stuck at my dining room table, eating my way through a jar of peanut butter and staring off into space. Not space actually, 'cause even in the dark, I could see Petunia Biggars's bicycle with its basket and chain.

What did the Upgrades say about her stealing stuff that threatens national security?

I walked around the table to study the basket more closely.

Maybe, like they said, Petunia was in possession of stolen national secrets—and now I was. Maybe they will kill to get them back. They have guns, don't they?

I shook the chain and pulled at it; it was so tight I couldn't get my fingers under it. I tried but couldn't pull it over a corner.

Maybe I should get the bolt cutters I have out in the garage.

I looked out the kitchen doors and across the fifty feet of yard I would have to cross to get the tool.

I can do it. Not much chance the monkeys will see me. What if I run into the raccoon?

I decided against breaking it open. Not just because it wasn't my property, but also because it seemed, in spite of the fact that Petunia had left it on my porch, that it didn't have anything to do with me. I might have decided to keep it safe for her, but in the end, whatever it was, it was someone else's problem, hers mainly. I mean, in spite of those pictures of me near her, in spite of my having been at the Blacks Only meeting, in spite of a vague memory of a guardian angel Petunia looking out for us when everyone else was shouting and angry, in spite of her showing up her to save me, in spite of all that, I had also been told quite emphatically by the frontline troops of Blacks Only to sit down and shut up. I could see no reason not to do as I was told. Even in the dark, in my own house, when I might have let my curiosity get the better of me, message received. No Samsons wanted. I dropped the chain and sat back down to make myself another peanut butter cracker sandwich.

Now, you're thinking that this is all bullshit, that there's no way I sat back and did nothing about any of this, that I've known all along where this was leading, back to Blacks Only, and that I didn't want to come straight out with it because it would ruin a good story. You're thinking that I absolutely must have recognized Petunia when she put her hand on my chest. She was just too special not to be identified and remembered. And that I am actually switching things up to make the story better, to have a mystery woman add some suspense, to prove that I actually am a writer.

Except that that's not me. I'm the opposite. I'm not one of those writers who's always looking at everything that happens to me as something that would make a good story. I don't cannibalize my life like the workshops told me I would. At least not yet. It takes me longer to put the pieces together, to see what's what.

Like Blacks Only. And Petunia. And Shemahn. And Ja'K. And the meeting where the deep state took those pictures.

I don't remember whose idea it was that we go, not mine for sure, probably not Ja'K's either, so that leaves Shemahn, although it doesn't really seem like her. I mean, she doesn't like crowds. She performs in front of thousands of people but only when there's a clear boundary between her and the fans; she can take them one at a time, but she can't stand the crush of fame. Maybe she has claustrophobia, agoraphobia, or the like. I don't know. I never asked her.

Anyway, we were at her house one night a few weeks back, brainstorming and trying to latch onto any bit of story that could be worked into something. She didn't want something that had been done to death—like slavery or autism or incurable cancer—she wanted something more uplifting and positive.

I said

What about that Malala? The one who won that peace prize.

The girl shot by the Taliban for trying to get an education?

She said.

That's the one.

No one's gonna believe me as a Pakistani schoolgirl struggling against the Islamic patriarchy.

Okay. Well, it doesn't have to be her exactly. It could be someone like her ...

Like Mukhtar Mai?

Mukhtar who?

The Pakistani woman who was raped to avenge the alleged crime of her twelve-year-old brother. She refused to commit suicide and now is working to educate Pakistani girls.

Shemahn barely looked up from her phone while she rattled off the thumbnail.

Refusing to commit suicide could be what wins the Oscar.

Not for me though.

She listed her objections:

First of all, I will not go to Pakistan for any reason—not for research, not to meet her, not for the shoot. No way. I'm boycotting nations that do that to women. And also, I don't think that an African American woman should be playing a Pakistani with all that head-wobbling memsahib stuff.

I think that's India.

Well, it doesn't matter. It's still an accent, not my strong suit, and it would seem racist.

Okay, what about Mary McLeod Bethune? I was reading about her online. She could—

That won't work. I won't be able to put on all that weight and still tour.

Tour while we're shooting?

Shemahn laughed.

Of course.

Eyes on her screen, she waved her scrolling finger around to indicate all the stuff that she didn't need to look at to know was there for her.

Have to pay for all this somehow, don't I?

I went back to the web, typed in "forgotten black women," and started reading. Shemahn got a text from a friend telling her to get off her "fat ass" and come to a Blacks Only meeting.

She wants to know what's my excuse?

She looked at me and at Ja'K, but we couldn't come up with one.

Ja'K headed off to get her bodyguard out of his room, but Shemahn stopped him.

No. Let Hassam sleep. He was up all last night with his youngest. We'll take Samson's car.

Oh no

I said, remembering how filthy my Prius was, inside and out

My car's full of all kinds of crap. And besides, Hassam would want you to wake him.

I don't care

Shemahn said

I've been around crap before. Crap is good. Crap is less conspicuous.

I was throwing stuff from the back seat into the way back and starting to have serious concerns about driving a millionaire pop star to a Blacks Only meeting.

You know, maybe there's a story for us in Blacks Only, Shemahn, but I really think you and Hassam should go, just the two of you. Not me—and not Ja'K either.

What do you mean? You're the writer. This is research. You're coming.

Don't get me wrong, but we don't belong at a Blacks Only meeting. Name says it all. It's an important statement. We should honor it.

But Shemahn wouldn't hear of it.

Fuck Blacks Only. Even though they're throwing shade at all that white-washed racial history, it's just as bad for us as Whites Only. Look around. What's that even mean anymore?

That black people can take care of themselves, solve their own problems.

I'm black, aren't I?

Yes.

And you solved my problem. You saved my life, didn't you?

I hemmed and hawed.

Hmm ... sort of. Look, I appreciate you describing what I did that way, but really, Shemahn, you probably wouldn't have died. You might've gotten hurt but not killed. Besides, I was just doing my job—and you had more to do with how it turned out than I did.

Well, I don't know anything that's proved that we *all* need each other better than that.

I'm sure there are better examples.

We don't need better examples. We need *any* examples so all those people in power can see that doing their job includes taking care of black people too. Now get in.

That settled it. In Bel Air anyway, but not in Baldwin Hills. The meeting was another matter entirely. None of the people in that church thought that research for Shemahn gave me a pass. In fact, I would say that they were openly and understandably hostile to all of us: Shemahn for bringing me and Ja'K and me for just being.

Fuck you, redneck scum! Get the fuck out of here, FBI pig! Ain't you already killed enough of us to make America great again?

Those were the kinds of things they shouted, but most of the anger wasn't verbal. Most of it was shoulders in the back and chest bumps.

Shemahn did her best to defend me.

Hey, stop it. Samson is here to help.

They weren't interested.

Fuck his help. We'll watch our own backs. We will rise. They can't kill all of us.

Samson's not the man.

Of course he's the man. He was born with a white stick up his ass.

They pressed in, pinning the three of us into corner next to a spinning rack of addiction pamphlets that we tripped over as we fought to keep our balance.

Shemahn kept shouting for her friend, but the friend didn't materialize.

Blacks Only! Blacks Only! Blacks Only!

I hope you bought your cinematic immunity card.

I grinned at Ja'K. He was a deer in the headlights, made more frightened by my gallows humor.

Cinematic what? Was I supposed to get a shot?

He was panicking, frantic for some promise of safe passage out of the press of angry African American faces.

Out of the corner of my eye, I noticed one woman who was not screaming. Although I couldn't be certain, she seemed to be actively eavesdropping on our conversation. I didn't have time to shoo her off. I had to keep Ja'K calm.

Immunity. And you don't get it from a shot. It's more like a force field. Just tell anyone who asks you what the fuck you're doing that you're with the movie and shazam, they can't touch you. That's cinematic immunity.

What movie? There's no movie.

There's *always* a movie.

At this, the eavesdropping woman stepped out of the crowd. Now, two days later, recognizable in memory, Petunia Biggars redirected the anger from me to the celebrity.

Who the fuck do you think you are, Shemahn? Fuck you. You don't belong here any more than they do.

I lowered my eyes and crossed my arms.

What the fuck are you even doing? Acting like you care about us. We're the ones living with the man's boot on our necks—not you.

As soon as the crowd stopped screaming about me and started booing Shemahn, I felt her celebrity charisma dimming. Even though she was stung by this personal indictment, she hadn't given up on her good intentions.

You trying to tell me that you've got everything so handled you don't need anyone's help? We all have a part in this story.

Petunia really let her have it.

As far as we're concerned, you're more of a problem than this asshole. You're part of the 1 percent that's keeping the whole system running. You're up there in your Bel Air mansion making all the racists feel good for having a black celebrity friend in the neighborhood when actually all you're doing is putting the shine on their boots so the real brothers and sisters don't see how fucked things are!

Fuck cinematic immunity, I thought. We should have brought Hassam.

C'mon, Shemahn. I think we've done enough research.

I took her arm and pulled her back in the direction we'd come from. But she didn't move. Or couldn't. Not that it matters which it was. It had the same result: another attack from Petunia.

What the fuck's the matter with you, girl? Listen to the man—get the fuck out of here.

Shemahn would not.

I tried pleading with the crowd, speaking to no one in particular since I wasn't making any eye contact, but pitching my voice to the same level as Petunia's.

I think she might be having a panic attack. Maybe if you could give us a little room.

Petunia had no sympathy for celebrity panic.

Who the fuck cares about some 1 percent hypochondriac's mental problems? We're the ones getting shot in the back. We're the ones who gotta panic!

Suddenly, Petunia took a very quick step toward me, and in the instant of taking that step, she lowered her voice so that only I could hear her.

Get your little research party out of here before these people stop listening to me.

A second later, Petunia shouted

I said leave, bitch!

She pushed Shemahn straight into me.

I didn't have to be told twice. I wrapped one arm around Shemahn, and using all my strength and Ja'K as a battering ram, I pushed us toward the door, all the time keeping my eyes on the ground and my mouth moving.

Excuse us. Pardon us. Sorry. Sorry.

I don't know how she did it, but Petunia did hold their attention long enough for us to get out of that meeting and back to my Prius. I didn't appreciate what she'd said about Shemahn enabling oppression, but I did know when to be grateful.

On the car ride back along Sunset Boulevard, Shemahn didn't have much to say, but she wasn't texting on her phone as usual. She was staring out the window.

Ja'K was blabbering away about how amazed he was by the strength of cinematic immunity and how he couldn't wait to test it out again. He flexed his biceps.

I had no idea!

At the house, I didn't follow them inside. I stayed by my car, hoping Shemahn had forgotten about me as she headed toward her front door.

She hadn't.

Thanks, Samson. You're right. There's a movie in Blacks Only. I'm sure of it.

Okay

I waved

I'll work on it.

As you know, my working on it was nothing to write home about. The way I saw it, applying the rules I'd learned in workshop to whatever had happened to us at that meeting didn't equal three acts. A scene maybe. Maybe even a good one, but not a movie that would win an Oscar for anyone. The only plot with more than one act that had come from that whole night was me getting mixed up with an activist on the run from the government and her bicycle basket full of who knows what, maybe pilfered secrets, maybe clown confetti. Nothing life changing for Shemahn.

Maybe, I thought, I should start with that transgender kid like Ja'K wants and find Shemahn a real part earlier on. Not Mrs. Muir or another Whitney Houston in *The Preacher's*

Wife, maybe something tragic, significant. Maybe I could avoid the nonsense. Maybe his dictation could unblock *me*,

In the morning—when I could open my laptop without giving myself away.

But that could be hours from now. I couldn't just sit there waiting for the sun to rise. Maybe this time in the dark wouldn't necessarily be wasted. Some writers said their best ideas had come to them when they just let their minds wander, like when they were stuck in traffic on the way home from work or when they were listening to some boring speaker in an orientation. Maybe if I stayed at the table and ate my way through the jar of peanut butter and box of saltines, I could free-associate my way from nonsense to genius. I decided not to consider moving to the couch to lean my head back and close my eyes. I would keep my eyes open until I saw what Shemahn needed me to see.

The problem with that intention was that what I saw was not a plot but Petunia's bicycle and basket.

Who was I kidding? I had to know what was in there!

It felt like one of those scenes in a movie where everyone knows there's a ticking bomb under the table except the person about to be blown to smithereens. Except in this fuckin' movie, the victim knows there's a bomb but *still* isn't allowed to do anything. Fuck that! If a bomb's about to go off under your table, nobody can tell you to sit down and shut up because this bomb is their business, not yours. A bomb in your house, even a house that should be torn down, is always your business.

I got up and put more muscle into pulling the chain off, but muscle wasn't enough. Petunia had done a damn good job of making sure of that. Without the key to that lock, there was no Samson way in. And bolt-cutters were out of the question, I realized, because however I got into this basket, if there were really stolen national secrets inside it, I would have to be able to deny I had seen them: cutting the chain wouldn't give me plausible deniability.

In the dark, I ran my fingers over and under the basket, trying to visualize a weakness in its construction. The bottom was a solid piece of wood like the lid. The lid had leather hinges that attached it, but the bottom didn't have any leather. It had to be attached somehow. I found the first Phillips-head screw with my pinkie.

Where is my screwdriver?

I pictured all my tools neatly arranged on my tool bench in the garage. My tool bag with all the stuff I took to the set on the ground. Even my Makita with its charger light glowing to indicate it was fully charged. Everything where it should be just not where I needed it at the moment.

I went to the kitchen and rummaged around in the drawers, but I didn't find a screwdriver. I did find a cheese knife that seemed pointy enough to do the trick, but I couldn't get the leverage right; the first screw didn't budge. I tried another. And then another. They were all in way too tight. I made my way around the basket a second time, pushing harder, but all the time worrying that the knife would slip and scar the basket. It could have been another case of me doing my own stunts and hurting myself—but then I remembered the Leatherman I had given Hildy for Christmas years ago. She'd thrown it in her drawer without taking it out the package. It was right where she left it.

Even with the Leatherman, it took me a long time to loosen the screws enough so the bottom of the basket fell down on the chain. I poked the Leatherman pliers through the gap I'd made and pulled out pieces of paper covered with charts and numbers I couldn't read in the dark. I took the papers into the bathroom, sat down on the toilet with a robe tented over my head, and used the flashlight on my phone to read them. Although when I say read them, don't think I mean I understood them. It was all meaningless data to me: columns listing compounds and bacteria and chemicals, followed by amounts and percentages. I knew it was a lab report, but about what wasn't clear. Nor was it clear how this info constituted any national secret since the scientist who had written the report worked at the DWP.

How could Dr. Harry Lime, senior water analyst at the Los Angeles Department of Water and Power, have info that could be a threat to national security?

Wednesday, 7:17 a.m.

Even though I didn't have an easy answer to the question, after all the trouble I had gone through to see what was in Petunia's basket, it seemed like a good idea to keep the report until I did. Not so it would give me away though.

It took me the rest of the night to make a copy and then put the basket back the way I'd found it—originals slid back through gap, bottom back on, screws nice and tight. I carried my desktop copier into my closet and tented it with a bunch of blankets so the flash of the tube wouldn't give me away to the Upgrades. I almost suffocated myself in the process, but I got it done.

As the first light of the dawn reached my windows, I was putting the finishing touches on my found object masterpiece: P. Biggars's Bike as Representation-of-America's-Abandoned-Home-Exercise-Equipment-Repurposed-as-Display-of-Unwanted-Gifts-Dirty-Clothes-

and-Dusty-Hats-Found-Art-Installation. The bike was good and hidden if you didn't know what you were looking for. I was betting the Upgrades didn't.

I walked to the front window to check that I hadn't inadvertently given myself away. The SUV was no longer parked in front of my house, which I had mixed feelings about. I put my dirty Carhhartts back on, went out to the sidewalk, and looked down my street in both directions. No black SUV anywhere, only my neighbors' cars and a few early risers out walking their dogs. The street was quiet, normal, but it didn't convince me that things were actually the way they should be. I remembered the sound that had woken me up and decided to walk around my house to investigate.

The first time around, I didn't notice anything unusual, and that was not because I was a clueless homeowner. Remember, I'm the one who stripped the Chinese drywall; but I'm not just Mr. Demolition. I know how things are supposed to be. I know where the gas shutoff is for after an earthquake. I know where the sump pumps are if it ever rains again. I know where the cable from the DirectTV comes off of the satellite along the gutter, down the front of my house and through a hole in the exterior wall you can see from the street. I've always hated the way the installers did that, as if the fact that you couldn't see the cable when you were inside the living room meant it wasn't visible from anywhere. If I'd been living there when it happened, I would have torn them a new one.

It was this sorry DirectTV cable that didn't jibe with my memory. I went back around a second time. Now, instead of one cable that disappeared into the wall behind the TV, there were two bundled together; the second one continued down the wall and disappeared into the crawl space. This second one looked legit, so I wasn't sure if I wasn't supposed to have two. I got a ladder and climbed up onto the roof to check out the dish. Nothing obviously wrong there. I went back down to the crawl space and poked at the cover. Except for the new cable, nothing seemed out of the ordinary. I pulled the cover off and stared at the black hole. I knew what I had to do, but I didn't want to for one obvious reason: the monster hairy rabid raccoon nesting in the darkness.

You'll remember that no exterminator had ever crawled under the house, but I might have forgotten to add that I hadn't bravely gone where no man had gone before either. And it's not like I hadn't been under plenty of houses in my day. I just didn't jump at the chance to meet my raccoon nemesis in the Cu Chi tunnels of Mar Vista. Who would? You? Not likely. There was only me. And I'm no Willem Dafoe in *Platoon*.

Still, I had to crawl under the house. I accepted that, but I wasn't going to go in there unprotected. I went back inside and layered up—fleece jacket from *Acid Trip*, Carhartt jacket from *The Last Long Shots*, heavy boots, glove liners, leather gloves, neoprene face mask, goggles. I had so many clothes on I could barely lift my arms to put on my hair helmet. Hair helmet? You're saying, get over yourself, Sam. Listen to the Ex for once. Regrowing your hair can't always be your priority, but wait a second, hear my logic before you jump on the bash-Sam bandwagon. First, I needed something to protect my head, and it's not like I had my old Titans high school football helmet handy. Second, of course, I didn't think the red flashing lights of the lasers were going to blind my nemesis, but I did think they might confuse it. And frankly, when you're fighting nature, you need every advantage.

So, with helmet lights flashing, my putter in one hand, and my biggest Maglite in the other, I flopped on my back next to the hole and started edging my way in. It was slow going, tracing the cable and crabbing backward. I had to stop every few feet, crane my head around, and shine a light into the recesses of the crawl space to look for the nest.

I was a couple of body lengths under the house with nothing rabid in sight when I traced the cable to a small black box attached to the subfloor. Weird. The box seemed like it belonged on the back of a TV and not exposed to dust and vermin under a house. There were a whole bunch of blinking green lights on the side and a spider web of tiny wires coming out of a central port on the bottom. I was looking for a way to free the box from the joist when I heard a couple of women talking loudly out in my front yard. I figured they were just passing by, so I didn't give them a second thought as I gathered up the spider web of wires with the idea of ripping them out. That was when I realized those passersby weren't passing. They were talking to me.

Young man!

I looked between my legs. Backlit faces shouted at me in the opening I had just crawled through.

May we have a minute of your time?

Can you come back later, I'm kinda busy

I shouted back.

I tried digging my fingers behind the box and then reconsidered and jerked my hand away like I'd been shocked. Fuck, I thought, what if it's a booby trap?

Please, we're here to save you.

Save me, I thought. Did she actually say that?

I crabbed myself around and started backstroking out of the crawl space. I was pretty confident by then that my nemesis did not live under my house, so what would a few minutes matter when I wasn't entirely sure what to do about the box anyway?

When I poked my head out of the vent, I found myself staring up at two grandmotherly African American women: one round like a beach ball and the other as thin as a toothpick. The two of them were bobbing and smiling at me like a pop-up Hallmark card. The halo of sun around their faces made me blink and squint, but with every other bob, I could see their smiles and the outlines of the Bibles in their hands as they gestured at me. Considering what I was wearing, I'm surprised they didn't take one look at me and run. 'Course they were on a mission.

We have come to save you, young man

One said.

Will you be saved?

The other echoed.

Really? I thought. That's what they meant? Fuckin' evangelicals trying to convert me? I would have been more aggressive if they weren't elderly and cute. Although they did remind me of the "pickalittle talkalittle" ladies from *The Music Man.*

I'm sorry. I'm not really a believer, and you can see that I'm—

It does not matter what you have believed or not believed in the past, young man. It is what you will believe in the future. That's all that the Lord cares about

Beach Ball intoned.

It is often the busiest man who is most in need of saving

Toothpick added.

We've been sent to you. You need to listen to us.

Beach Ball had the last word.

This isn't exactly the best time.

I tried again to put them off.

I'm flat on my back … this is kind of inconvenient.

What time is not inconvenient? No time!

Toothpick said.

What time can we afford not to be saved? No time!

Beach Ball said.

Okay,

I said, resigning myself to the inevitable, scooching myself out of the hole, and getting back to my feet. I pulled off the goggles and the neoprene mask and brushed the dirt off my clothes.

Knock yourself out.

Funny you should use that word

Beach Ball said.

When the messenger of the Lord knocks on a man's door, it is the messenger that has something to tell him—not he who is crawling in the darkness who should be talking back.

Toothpick thumped her Bible on my chest as she spoke. She was stronger than I expected a toothpick to be.

For what could he in his ignorance have to say to her? When the Lord's messenger knocked on your door—

Stop. This is way too specific. What Lord's messenger ever knocked on my door?

Toothpick paid no heed to my objection.

When the messenger stood on your threshold, you sent her away. The messenger did not seek a promise from you. She only sought to bring you the good news, a promise of redemption through the truth.

Hold your horses, ladies!

I grabbed the top of the Bible to stop the pummeling and looked around to make sure the Upgrades weren't hiding in the bushes.

You mean Petunia Biggars? She's the Lord's messenger? If that's who you're talking about, I want to get the story straight. I didn't turn her away. I told her she could wait on the porch while I called the cops.

It is written that we should render unto Caesar what is Caesar's, but sometimes when it is a matter of life and death, the cops will not suffice. We must save ourselves.

Beach Ball whacked me on the head with her Bible to punctuate her declarations.

As I rubbed the bump, it finally dawned on me that these two grandmothers had been sent by Blacks Only to assault me for turning Petunia away, but I wasn't going to take it lying down.

Look, I'm sorry. I didn't recognize her, but even if I had, why would I let her into my house? She should have gone to the police if she really needed help. Hey, I saved her bike for her. Tell her anytime she wants, it's waiting for her.

The messenger has no need for a bicycle, my son. A bicycle is not a spiritual vehicle.

Tell me what to do with it then—or send her to fetch it.

Toothpick choked up.

No one fetches anything from beyond the grave.

Beach Ball choked up too.

It's up to us, all of us, but you in particular, my son, to carry on her good work.

What?

The messenger has passed, my son.

Toothpick pulled her Bible back over her heart.

What? Those asshole Upgrades got her?

Run down by a TV executive on PCH. Police claim she was higher than a kite.

So, it was an accident, I mean, a *real* accident? She wasn't murdered?

Beach Ball shook her head.

Oh, no, my son. It was no accident. The messenger does not do drugs.

The Lord giveth, and the Lord taketh away

Toothpick said.

But He still shows us the path of righteousness

Beach Ball added.

She's dead?

Fuck! I couldn't believe what I was saying—or how it shook me. Before I knew it, the grandmothers had trapped me in a massive hug, pinning my arms to my sides so that I could not wipe away my tears.

I'm really sorry. I should have helped her.

I fought off the blubbering.

No, my son, you are not to blame. You are to be thanked.

Are you kidding me?

I pushed them away.

Thanked for shutting the door in her face?

No! Thanked, for you are to carry on her work.

What?

I was really confused.

They preached rapid-fire, talking over each other.

You must be careful.

The devil is watching.

They were nodding importantly as if what they were saying was obvious.

The devil has more ways to keep his eye on us than we can know.

His minions are out to get you.

They ping-ponged back and forth.

Even when you think you've blinded his last eye, he'll open another.

But he will not succeed. You will resist him. We thank you for that.

He won't?

He will not!

I will?

You will!

You do?

Praise the Lord!

They were speaking so quickly I didn't know what to make of it.

You have everything you need.

I do?

Yes. She entrusted all to you.

All is what?

The truth!

A whole basket of it!

What the fuck?

They turned and walked away, but Beach Ball called back to me

You have crawled out of your hole and into the light, young man. She was right to choose you to spread her truth.

Okay. I guess. Hey, what do I do with her bike?

Ride, my son.

Ride? Where?

To Kingdom Come.

Where is that, I thought. Not in Los Angeles.

And if we were you, we'd get a dog

Beach Ball said.

To be on the safe side

Toothpick said enthusiastically

A large one with a loud bark and lots of sharp teeth!

Why?

They didn't answer. They didn't have to. It was a stupid question. They had come here to save me, hadn't they? And it wasn't from sin—it was from the bad guys who had killed Petunia. A dog was a good idea.

I watched them cross the street and walk up the path to my neighbor's front door. They rang the doorbell and waited patiently with the Bibles pressed to their breasts. After a short interval when no one opened the door, they walked to the next house and rang that doorbell.

They worked their way down the street from house to house, chatting and laughing with each other to keep up the charade. They did not once look back at me. It was like I had imagined the whole thing.

Except that I hadn't, none of it. Not Petunia or the Upgrades or the grandmothers. They were all part of something, a conspiracy, that was more life-threatening than being a professional stuntman. You're thinking that I should have gone to the police at this point. With what? A dead girl's bicycle and a basketful of lab reports that didn't mean anything?

Thanks for coming in, Mr. Agonistes.

I could hear the brush-off already.

No, you don't need to leave the bike or the papers. We know how to find you.

Nope. Watching the Grannies turn the corner and disappear, I knew exactly what I—what Samson—had to do to carry on Petunia's work. It was time to pay a visit to Dr. Harry Lime, senior DWP analyst. Was I scared? Sure. Did I know what I was getting into? Not a clue. But I couldn't just lock myself up in my house and wait for them to come get me.

Remember, I'm the guy who does all his own stunts.

Wednesday, 10:00 a.m.

It had never occurred to me until I stood in the lobby of the DWP building that the best place to hide a national secret might not be in a vault guarded by Navy SEALs but somewhere in a vast bureaucratic labyrinth, deep in a nondescript, nonthreatening complex on Venice Boulevard in Los Angeles. Okay, maybe it had occurred to me, but I'd forgotten it. I did see *Raiders of the Lost Ark*.

Outside the DWP was a mostly empty, buckled asphalt parking lot surrounding a building in the middle of acres of dry nothing. I'd driven by hundreds of times and never noticed it. Inside, there wasn't any security, no metal detectors or guards, no signs with arrows or room numbers, there wasn't even a receptionist to ask you what you were doing or point you down one of the dozens of identical, no rhyme or reason, empty white hallways, endless corridors radiating into scary nowhere. Someone had been killed because of the report I had in my pocket, so I wasn't being paranoid to think my own life was also in danger. This wasn't *Raiders;* this was *THX 1138*. However, as daunting as that was, I, Samson, wasn't daunted. I was sliding down the knife's edge and focused only on making Senior Analyst Dr. Harry Lime in Room 102 reveal his secrets. I chose a hallway at random and set off.

After fifteen minutes of walking under identical banks of fluorescent lights, past identical, unmarked metal doors, and meeting no one, it occurred to me that it would be pure luck if the way I was headed led to Lime and equally pure luck if after I found him, I could then find my way back out to my car.

This is what the devil had in mind all along, I thought. Send your pilgrim into a labyrinth from which he could not escape. No string, no breadcrumbs. I could starve to death.

I broke out in a cold sweat. I almost decided to just sit down and wait to be found, but I knew that could be never. I kept going. Every time I turned a corner and headed down a new corridor, I felt myself getting farther and farther from the real world. Whether or not it was smart, I started trying every doorknob and knocking on every door. None of the knobs turned; no door opened. I shuffled along more and more slowly and tried not to panic.

Hey … Hey …

I called, loud enough to be heard but not so loud as to set off alarm bells

Can I get some help? I think I'm lost.

At a T in the road, I started to turn right, thought better of it, and went left. I found something different, a door with a sign on it: Room 101. It was not Lime's room, but anything new felt like progress. This time, I banged on the door with my fist until I heard a man's voice.

Stop that!

I was too relieved to have found a human to obey. I banged harder.

I'm lost. I need help.

This is not lost and found.

I'm looking for Dr. Harry Lime.

Never heard of him.

Is Room 102 close to here?

No, of course not.

This is 101.

It is not.

That's what the sign says.

If this were Room 101, there wouldn't be a sign, would there?

The door is very clearly marked.

In what language?

Numbers.

The man on the other side of the door shouted to someone else

Hey, Orson, there's some idiot saying there are numbers on the door. Can you believe it?

I couldn't hear Orson's answer but it was relayed to me.

Orson says there are lots of numbers.

Okay, then ask Orson if he knows where 102 is.

He's in the middle of something.

Please!

I heard an exaggerated sigh and then an unintelligible mumble, which was followed by a pronouncement:

Orson says to tell you, if he were looking for something, he'd go back.

What the fuck does that mean?

I pounded harder on the door. No response. The man was gone. I looked both ways down the corridor.

Which way is back? His back or my back?

Even after a career in the movies, I still had trouble with the difference between camera right and camera left, but this was worse. Where is back in an undefined spatial universe? Who could say? I just picked one: my past, my back.

Why not? I thought, I can't be more lost than I already am.

And it was good that I did. A hundred yards back in the corridor I'd just come down was a sign for Room 102. How had I not seen it?

I turned the knob, expecting more frustration, but the door miraculously opened into a vast lab. It was more or less the same colorless white as the halls, but this one looked like a high school chemistry class. It was filled with lab tables and machinery and two scientists, a man and a woman, total pencil-neck geeks, about my age, the guy half my weight, the woman even less, wearing long lab coats and puttering around, peering into microscopes, swirling colored liquids in beakers, lighting Bunsen burners, basically too preoccupied with science to notice me.

Full of gratitude for not being lost forever, my composure restored, my cover story rehearsed, I walked up to the younger, female scientist and said

I'm looking for Dr. Harry Limes.

I added the S to his name and hissed it be annoying. Both scientists stopped what they were doing and stared at me, but neither one spoke until the male gulped like a fish out of water.

It's Lime, singular, not Limes, plural. I'm Dr. Lime.

Nice to meet you, Harry.

I put on the local yokel and held out the photocopies.

I reckon these belong to you.

He took the papers, glanced at them, turned a whiter shade of white than he already was, glared at me, took a minute to rub the bridge of his nose, and said

This is a photocopy.

It is?

Where's the original?

Beats me, Doc. That's all I git.

There are also pages missing: 3, 4, 7. Where are they?

Like I said, Doc. That's all I git.

Git? How exactly did you *git* these?

That's the damndest thing. Inside my DWP bill. In the US mail. Can you believe it?

That was the story I had come up with on my drive over from Mar Vista.

I thought about just throwin 'em away, but then I saw your name down there, Dr. Harry Limes, senior analyst.

I couldn't help trolling him with the S again.

I could see it was kinda important. I thought maybe you'd accidentally put them in my bill, you know, the way folks do sometimes, mix things up they shouldn't have, but they seemed important all covered with numbers and the like, so naturally I thought you'd want 'em back. In case they was important, like I said, you know. I think it's the responsibility of every American, you know, to see something and then say it. Sorry, I mean, you know, kinda of nervous meeting a senior analyst for the first time ever and such, you know, if you see something, say something. That's it.

Even though I was blabbering nonstop, I was watching Harry closely. The way he was sweating and crumpling the report in his fist, it seemed like Petunia really had been onto something.

What is it, Harry?

The female geek snuck a peek at the papers and then snapped her attention to me. I think if she hadn't been wearing such thick bottle-lens glasses, she would have been staring daggers. Although she was hardly intimidating since she looked like Jerry Lewis in *The Nutty Professor.*

Nothing, Holly. Just some irrelevant reports. Old data. I wonder how these slipups happen.

Slipups—that's exactly the word I was thinking of. That's exactly what's wrong with this country, wouldn't you say, all the slipups right, left, and center?

While I was talking, Harry was removing his lab coat, putting on a greasy blue Izod windbreaker, vintage 1972, stuffing the report in his pocket, and heading for the door. I stayed as close to him as I could without making it obvious.

Not that I'm asking, but do you think there'd be some kind of reward for being a good citizen and all? What with the drought, water costing what it does, and all anybody's got to—

Lime ignored me.

I just realized I'm late for an appointment, Holly. Lock up when you leave.

I heard the door latch click behind me.

Well, I, for one, am certainly glad I could get those papers back to their rightful owner. And if there's no chance of getting something off on my bill, it was sure nice to meet you, Dr. Holly, and see what great work the DWP is doing.

Holly's glare dialed up from daggers to laser beams, but I slipped out of the door and into the hallway in time to see Lime hotfoot it around the corner.

I took off after him, running as quietly as I could in the empty corridors. I could hear Lime's nervous walk/shuffle/run ahead of me. I was counting on keeping him in earshot since there weren't other people around to hide among. And that worked mostly. Now and then, I caught a glimpse of his blue windbreaker before he rounded the next corner and confirmed I was still following the right guy. I didn't know where he was leading me. Could we be on our way out? Could we be heading deeper into the labyrinth—to some room where I will find out what the numbers on the report mean but at the cost of my life?

I tried not to dwell on the idea of being taken by some sinister force, locked away and forgotten by everyone except my kids who would be forced to live the rest of their lives wondering what happened to their dad. Okay, maybe they wouldn't wonder; they'd know. Hildy would be sure I'd bitten off more than I could chew. Atticus would say I was all hat no cattle.

Then I heard the walk/shuffle/run slow and stop, followed by a metallic click and then the slam of a heavy door being sucked closed by a difference in air pressure.

Outside, I thought as I turned the corner. Finally! Now I can follow Lime safely.

Of course, who was I kidding? Nothing about it was as easy as that—or safe for that matter. The hallway I was staring down, unlike most of the hallways I had seen, had many doors, at least six, on both sides, so it was impossible to know which one he'd gone out. It was also impossible to know whether one of them would put me somewhere I'd rather not be, but it wasn't like I had a choice.

The longer I waited, the farther away he got. I ran from one door to the next, turning the knobs and putting my shoulder into them until I had tried them all. None of them opened. I was stuck. I'd found and lost Lime and still didn't have any clue what was going on. I sank to the floor with my back against the last door I had tried.

What the fuck do I do now?

I remembered my cell phone and pulled it out.

Maybe there is someone to call: 911 or my Ex? How can I explain where I am so they can find me before the bad guys do?

As I slumped there, I heard a key going into a lock, and the door I'd been leaning against fell open. I scrambled to my feet and rushed into a blinding glare, not caring who had opened the door or what they might say to have a strange man bursting upon them. Technically speaking, the woman I ran into wasn't a stranger: it was the female scientist with the laser-beam glare. I got so tangled up with her that we both ended up in a heap in the sand of the desert landscaping that surrounded the building.

Sorry. I'm very sorry.

I got to my feet and pretended to help her as I tried to make my getaway. No dice. She had her nails dug deep into my bare forearms.

What did you do with her?

I don't know what you're talking about, Doc. I didn't do nothin' with no one.

Where did you get those water reports? Tell me the truth!

I pulled as hard as I could to get away, but I only succeeded in pulling her to her feet.

I did tell you the truth.

Did they get her?

The scientist seemed to be losing her shit.

Did they make her talk? They know about me, right? Right?

I don't know what anyone knows.

She dug her nails deeper and stared at me intently.

What's your name?

I didn't want to tell her.

Tell me your name! Is it Samson?

She raised her voice almost to a yell. I nodded. Her mind clicked.

One China, 7:00 p.m. Don't be late.

She let go of my arms, fell back in the sand, and shouted

Help me! Help me! He's getting away. Help me! Dr. Limes! Dr. Limes, watch out! He's after you!

Plural Limes, I thought. She's trolling him too. I didn't know why until she jerked her head to the left to indicate which direction I should be fleeing.

One confused blink later, I was running down the sidewalk as she continued her cries for help and her warnings to Dr. Limes. When I reached the parking lot, I kept my head down as I fast-walked to my car. Dr. Holly had stopped screaming but I didn't want to call too much attention to myself. My precaution was unnecessary. Even though

I tripped on a buckled piece of blacktop and nearly face-planted, no one ran out of the building to apprehend me.

The parking lot was deserted. My car wasn't surrounded. Clearly no one was alarmed. All the secrets were still where they were supposed to be. The morning had returned to being stiflingly hot and unremarkable. The Prius started, the air-conditioning blasting hot air in my face. I turned it off. The car went to the battery.

Then there was silence. Nothing moved.

Looking over my shoulder to make sure I wasn't being followed, I drove out the same way I had come in.

Wednesday, 12:00 p.m.

I headed toward the valley with no clear plan in mind but to keep moving. Considering what I'd just been through, almost being vanished with no trace, it's no surprise that I would want someone to talk to, but as you know, I didn't have a lot of options. My Ex wasn't the best listener but I took a chance and called her on the way over the Sepulveda Pass. It went straight to voice mail.

Serves me right, I thought.

I talked slowly, wanting to give her a clue without leaving any evidence.

Okay, sorry I missed you earlier. Haven't had a chance to listen to the messages yet either. Sorry. Been running around like crazy. Anyway, called you back instead. No new news on my end, but it'd be *good* to talk. Maybe you have news. I guess I can listen to your messages. 'Course, the only message that either of us wants is that Atticus is okay. And I kinda doubt that's why you called. Mostly I expect that you're just anxious. Ditto. Okay, well, then …

Right then, I saw the exit for the 101 to Ventura and decided to take a chance.

I'm headed out to see Hildy … to see if she knows anything … okay, great, talk later.

Hildy took one look at me and announced,

You'll have to wait. And if there's an emergency, then you can forget it. I won't have a minute for bullshit.

I waited, feeling oddly safe, standing by the glass front door, watching for the Upgrades or any other suspicious characters and listening to people behind me fuss over their pets. One woman, older than my long-dead granny, wearing a hat and white gloves, brought her barking Aussie shepherd over to tell me how she hadn't been able to train the dog not to bark at the neighbor's cat, the postman, the phone ringing, her son, the accountant—and me. It was hard to hear her over the barking, but I caught enough: Blue just loved her so much and didn't want anyone coming near her.

You're very lucky

I shouted because it seemed like the right thing to say, but I was wishing her away.

Do you have a dog?

Nope.

Dogs are wonderful. You should get one.

I'm not really a pet person.

This is the best dog I've ever had. The best.

So you said.

You should consider an Aussie. They're all named Blue by the way.

That's good to know. I wouldn't want to call a dog by the wrong name.

Why are you here if you don't have a pet?

To see my daughter. She's the veterinarian.

Your daughter's the veterinarian?

Blue upped his barking.

Yes.

She's very young.

I suppose so.

Blue does not bark at her.

That's lucky.

Hildy only reappeared after there were no more patients in her waiting room.

What do you want?

What makes you think I want anything?

I don't know—maybe the fact that none of my family ever comes to see me unless they do.

What did Atticus want?

I never said it was Peck.

You didn't have to. When was this?

She sighed heavily. Her expression was familiar: she didn't need this. Why couldn't her family work out their shit somewhere else? She must have decided it wasn't worth resisting.

Saturday. He needed a place to crash ... and to borrow some money.

Did he tell you Francesca kicked him out? That he walked off the job?

No. And I didn't ask questions. I figured he'd tell me what was going on if he felt like it.

Sure. Is he still staying at your place?

I would never let him stay with me. He doesn't flush the toilet.

Okay, but you loaned him money?

You and Mom should talk once in a while—or maybe you should take some parenting classes.

I ignored her dig.

Can you could stop being pissed off at me for long enough to tell me where your brother is?

I haven't seen him since yesterday morning. And I didn't *give* him money. I needed someone to stay overnight with an anxious patient. So, I paid Peck to do it.

That doesn't strike me as the smartest thing to do. What if something happened?

Something did.

Oh, I thought. It's not me she's pissed off at.

The dog he was looking after kind of freaked out and got her leg caught under the door of her cage. She ripped out all her stitches trying to get free. Nearly bled to death.

Christ! Where was your brother?

Not where I was paying him to be.

Did the dog make it?

Yes, but barely, I got to her in time.

Her owners must be pretty pissed.

She's a rescue. That's why she gets so anxious. Jogger found her tied to a lamppost in Hancock Park. She had a giant gash on her leg that had become infected.

That's fuckin' cruel. Why do people have dogs if they won't take care of them?

It's expensive.

The shelter pays you to stitch her up?

Hardly, Dad. They don't have any money.

You're a good person, Hildy.

Not always. And now, if you really don't want anything, I need to get back to paying my mortgage.

Another dig, but I ignored it because as I talked to her, I calmed down enough for my wheels to start turning.

Actually, I do.

She groaned. Whatever patience she had had for her father blurped out of the balloon.

Is that rescue still here?

Yes.

Can I see her?

Why?

She was suspicious, like she thought I was just stalling before I got to what I really wanted.

I'd like to offer emotional support.

Okay, but then you have to leave. I can't waste any more time with this.

She led me back through her clinic to a roomful of cages, big and small, stacked up along one wall. There was a fold-out cot across from the cages. And that was it. No TV. No phone. No equipment of any kind. Not much of an overnight ward.

This where Atticus was when she got her leg caught?

It was obvious to anyone what I was thinking: the kid must have been completely wasted not to have done something to help the dog.

Probably not. There's no Wi-Fi back here.

That his stuff there?

I sat down, picked up a canvas gym bag from under the cot, and started going through it.

That's an invasion of privacy

Hildy said, but that didn't stop me.

As it was, there wasn't much privacy to invade: jockstrap, bike shorts, some workout gloves, PowerBars, Red Bulls. At the bottom, shoved into a single athletic sock, I found what had to be a handgun. Not an Upgrade Glock—more like a *NYPD Blue* revolver. Hildy was watching my face as I recognized it. I pretended like I hadn't found anything, put everything back in the bag, and returned it to where I found it.

Hold it a second, you're thinking. I should have taken that gun. After all, I had a lot more reason to have a gun than my son did. My life was in danger. But I hate guns.

So, which one is she?

I asked.

Hildy pointed to the middle cage in the row of big cages at the bottom of the wall. I squatted down to try to see the dog, but it was like looking into the crawl space under my house. All I could make out was a mass of black fur and now and then, when she panted, some broken front teeth.

What is she?

Longhaired German shepherd.

Black? Aren't German shepherds brown and black? Rin Tin Tin, right?

There are black ones and white ones too.

How old do you think she is?

Old. I don't know exactly. She's a senior citizen—that's for sure.

What's her name?

No idea. She was abandoned, remember?

What's going to happen to her?

She'll go back to the shelter soon, today probably, and they'll try to find someone to take her.

What are her chances?

People usually don't adopt old dogs. They're kind of past their sell-by date.

Like your dad, I thought.

And if no one takes her?

Sooner or later, they'll bring her back here, and I'll put her down.

I stood up.

What if I take her?

This is how I am going to start to change her mind about me, I thought, while at the same time getting myself a dog with big teeth. Two birds, right?

Are you kidding? You're allergic to dogs.

I'm not allergic to dogs. Who told you that?

Mom. That's why we couldn't get a puppy.

Shit, I thought. How had I forgotten that particular parental lie?

Okay, well, that's partly true. I am sort of allergic. Or was. I think I've grown out of it. I've been around dogs on set, and it hasn't killed me.

Hildy half laughed. She wasn't buying it.

Look. I don't give a shit anymore about the lies you told us when we were kids, but I can't have you lying to me now.

Maybe you're just not a dog person. You really want to rescue this dog?

Yeah, I do.

She studied me for a minute.

Only if you tell me the real reason why. You think saving Shemahn certifies you as some endless do-gooder, Dad? Trust me, you can't Samson a dog. They see through our bullshit.

Funny thing you should mention Shemahn. I didn't actually save her.

Whatever, it doesn't matter. Why are you suddenly wanting to help this dog?

Because of your brother

I said and thought, three birds, even better.

Hildy stared at me for a long time, like she was trying to figure out what my real angle was, and then she gave up and walked out of the room.

I squatted and waggled my fingers through the cage at the dog like it was something I knew dogs liked. The dog didn't seem too interested.

Hildy rattled off everything she could think of as she helped me put the dog in the car.

Since I vouched for you, the shelter's okay with you taking her. On a trial basis. You'll need to stop and get some food and a bed. Here's an antibiotic she takes twice a day for the next ten days. Keep the cone on her so she doesn't pull out the stitches. Bring her back in two weeks, and I'll take them out. Call my vet tech, Trudy, if you have any questions. Oh, and if you really intend to adopt her, you probably ought to think of a name for her.

Won't that confuse her?

Maybe, but don't worry, you call her the same thing enough times, and she'll figure out you're talking to her. Kind of like giving her a nickname. People get new nicknames all the time. You answer to more than one name, don't you? Shepherds are smart. Too smart for their own good sometimes.

Petunia

I said.

Hildy seemed startled.

Where'd you pull that out of?

I pretended that I didn't know—mainly because I didn't have a reason that made sense. Even I didn't think naming a dog after a person made up for getting her killed.

Well, you and Petunia take care.

Hildy was smiling.

You too, Hildy, and if you hear from your brother or anything about where he might be, please call.

I will, Dad, but I know I won't. Peck's too far gone.

He's just lost, honey. Lots of people are lost. Look at Petunia here. She was lost, and now she is found.

No, Dad. Lost people have a chance of being found, of coming back to themselves, because they want that. Atticus doesn't want to be found—not by his family or Francesca or anyone normal anyway. Atticus likes who he is. He likes being Peck. He likes spending his time on the internet bullying people he's never met, women, minorities. No one can shut him up. And when he's not harassing people, he's watching porn. He's my brother, and I guess I love him, but he's a troll, Dad.

How the fuck did that happen?

You're asking me? You're his father.

Wednesday, 4:00 p.m.

Now you might have a problem with me naming this dog Petunia. Maybe you think it's quasi-racist for a white guy to name a black-haired dog after an African American woman who died in a mysterious way, perhaps at the hands of the police state. Or maybe you're wondering how I can be so sure she's dead. What happened to habeas corpus? Maybe she'd resent having her name abused. Or maybe what you're really wondering is if I believe that taking an unloved, worn-out dog into my house and naming her after the stranger I turned away could cure me of being a fragile phony?

I would have to say no. To the last one. I didn't think that naming this dog Petunia made up for a mistake I'd made, if it was one. I mean, of course, it was a mistake in the kind of cosmic sense. So, if it wasn't really to honor a person I hardly knew, then why not go with a name without baggage like Liesel or Gretchen—or Gretel, if I was determined to stay with the lost-and-found theme? I could've. I guess. And it wasn't too late to change my mind and go with something less charged. Except that it was too late. Too late for the murdered Petunia anyway. And maybe too late for me to take back a lifetime of me doing me.

What's done is done, I thought. The dog is named.

I didn't have a lot of experience with dogs, so I set Petunia's bed up in the front hall of the bungalow where I could keep an eye on her from wherever I was—and, more importantly, where she could see and be seen by anyone trying to break in. I figured the grandmothers were onto something with the barking, but I had no idea how to train a dog to guard a house. I spent a little time on the internet watching how-to videos, but they weren't much help. Not that I didn't see how it could work if you were patient and took your time, but I didn't have patience or time.

I made some lame attempts to provoke her to see if she had any bark in her: walking around outside the house, making burglar noises, and then peering inside to see what she did. From what I could tell, she didn't even lift her head off the bed. I tried louder noises to startle her, banging pots and trash cans, pounding on the walls and the front door. Still nothing. I started to think maybe she was deaf, but then when I checked that out, it was clear that even though she couldn't be bothered to lift her head and bark, she would roll her eyes in the direction of the noise I made.

At this point, I didn't really know what I was going to do. Not with Petunia. Petunia and I were a done deal. I was stuck with her—and she was stuck with me. I could only hope that once we got used to each other, her natural guard dog instincts would come barking back, but I didn't give that much thought. No, I was thinking about the bugging of my house and what I could do about the police state and whether or not it was safe for me to meet Dr. Holly at One China at seven o'clock.

Of course, from the police state's point of view, anyone who did not cooperate was a threat. Uncooperative described me pretty well, but the way I looked at it, even if they thought they had my best interests at heart, if they wanted to see into my house, even a teardown like mine, they had to go through proper channels and not just muscle their way past me. If it hadn't been for the church ladies, I probably would have escalated things by pulling out the wires, but I didn't. And the longer I considered the situation, the more I agreed with Toothpick and Beach Ball. No matter how many times you poke out the devil's eye, he'll always grow another. Better to know what he's looking at than not.

Petunia signed off on the plan when I sat down on the floor in front of her, took the cone in my hands, and explained my nightmare at the DWP. The seriousness in her brown eyes told me she couldn't believe how close I had come to never getting out of there; there wasn't a doubt in my mind that she'd had a similar experience herself at least once.

So, with some time to kill till dinner, I went back to my real life, trying to write a critically acclaimed vehicle for Shemahn. Even without a deadline, I knew my time was running out. And not because Shemahn was fickle and ungrateful—but because the realities of Hollywood and her creative future were knocking on her door. Sooner or later, she would have no choice but to let them in. If I didn't solve the problem of what would be her next project soon, she would have to shift me and our Samson partnership to the back burner and green-light something else. And even if another movie's green light was spun as a yellow for me, a long enough yellow eventually turned into red, and a red for me, the writer's-blocked working stiff, would never go back to green. Not to mention that Shemahn's bankability would also be tested by this other project. Untested she and I could make any movie we wanted, but one flop would turn our world upside down.

I sat on my couch with my computer on my lap and typed out a list of all the kinds of people who could interact with a transgender youth. Next, I typed out a list of all the creative ambitions a transgender youth might have. While I typed, I tried to imagine Ja'K encountering the people on my list or conveying his creativity to them through interpretative dance. I chose him for the obvious reason that I might have been tone-deaf to most of contemporary culture, but I could recognize someone's life story when it hit me over the head. I thought I was getting somewhere until I reread the list and realized how generic these types of people were, how overdone a movie would be if Shemahn played the harried teacher or the jaded musician or the doubting nun who nurtured the creative ambitions of a tragic youth. No. I needed something that hadn't been done to death.

What do you think, Petunia?

I looked up at her.

She might not have moved at the sound of my voice, but that was only because she was already staring at me intently out of the funnel of the white plastic cone.

You have any good ideas?

She did not, or not that she would share anyway, although I knew she was working on it.

You're wondering what I'm going to do. What's my next step? Am I too scared to go to Chinatown? Has Samson gone past up to his neck to in over his head?

I got up.

Don't answer that

I said as I stepped over her bed on my way to take a shit.

Petunia sighed heavily.

While I was in the bathroom, I did think of something I could do, not about the screenplay or Chinatown but how to fuck with the Upgrades. I took off all my clothes and went back out into living room. After a little pacing back and forth, pretending I was deep in thought, I started to do some yoga, downward dogs, child's poses, planks, and what have yous. I don't know a lot of yoga, but I thought the image of a dunlaped, flat-assed, naked middle-aged man was about as repulsive as you could get. Petunia didn't seem to mind, so I kept it up till my muscles ached. I tried one of those tree poses, but I couldn't get my balance, and then I did a handstand with my toes on the wall. All in all, I thought it would make for great thing to play at my trial.

The phone ringing startled me into falling out of the handstand and bruising my heel. I limped to the sofa to answer it.

What? Hello? What?

I feel your pain.

It was Ja'K.

Pain? What?

It's keeping you from writing, isn't it? You will miss the deadline, won't you?

Ja'K stayed on message. I had to give him that.

If you can't take it, I will bring in another writer until you're back on your feet.

I'm on my feet now.

I knew that once the door to another writer opened, mine would be closed.

How's it going then? It's been twenty-four hours. Are you done?

Getting there. It's coming.

After the head start we gave you, I don't understand what's taking so long.

I gritted my teeth and kept quiet.

Okay, well, listen, I just called to remind you that whatever you come up with, you have to show it to me before it goes to Miss Mahn. Google doc it to me.

Remind me? That's the first time I've heard that.

Well, that might be because I only just thought of it. This is your reminder.

But you're not my partner—she is.

Look, Samson, we all agree it's for the best that I'm in charge of the development.

I don't agree. And stop calling me Samson.

Ja'K ignored me.

Nonetheless, it's obvious that I'm the only one who understands what Miss Mahn needs. What I know is that she doesn't have time to waste on red herrings and wild MacGuffins.

And you've seen your share of those?

Certainly. I haven't gotten where I am not knowing how to tell a mule from a donkey.

You haven't gotten anywhere, Ja'K, I thought.

Okay, well, I have to go. There's someone at the door, but thanks for the heads-up.

I hung up. I was standing on my good foot and rubbing my bruised heel when the doorbell actually did ring. For a brief moment, it occurred to me that the Upgrades were using my own words as an excuse to send in a strike team. I snuck up to the door and peered through the peephole. Not a strike team. Not that kind anyway. It was my Ex.

She reached up and knocked, striking her closed fist on the door right next to the peephole and making me jump back.

Sam! Open up!

She shouted.

I'm not decent!

I shouted back.

I want to talk to you—I promise not to look at you!

I gave myself the once-over and decided to face the inevitable. I cracked the door, and she slipped through.

Christ

She said, fanning herself immediately,

It's a sweatbox in here, and it smells like …

She pointed at Petunia.

What the fuck is that?

Then, contrary to what she promised, she did turn to look at me, and her mouth really fell open. It wasn't attractive.

And what the fuck's with you? Don't tell me you've been sweating to the oldies.

I ignored the dig.

That's Petunia. Hildy let me rescue her.

The Ex walked over and peered down at the dog. Petunia did not bother to look up. Neither one of them made any effort to be friends.

What's wrong with her?

Besides having her leg sliced up and being abandoned and almost dying? Nothing.

Why isn't she doing things that dogs do when friendly people come up to them: barking, wagging, jumping?

Are you friendly?

She pffft-ed, slung her purse strap over her shoulder, and went to raise the blinds.

I ran to stop her.

Nope, nope, nope.

You have to get some air in here, Sam.

No! *You* have to get some air in here. I'm reducing all outside stimulation so I can focus.

Are clothes considered outside stimulation?

She gave me the once-over.

I don't know how I feel that my ex-husband walking around naked isn't a distraction anymore. Nothing to see here, folks, nothing to see.

Fuck off!

Don't be so sensitive.

I'm a lot older than I used to be.

Ain't that the truth. If you're not going to open the curtains, at least you could offer me something cold to drink. You got any beer?

On a weekday? Before five o'clock? Things aren't that bad, are they?

Not drunk bad, but beer bad, yes.

I pulled a six-pack of IPA out of the refrigerator, put it on the table, and popped the caps on two of them as she sat down. I maneuvered a chair around to where I could keep an eye on Petunia without being full frontal for my wife. The cool wood felt good on my bare ass cheeks.

Courtesy of Atticus, I assume?

Our boy Atticus.

I'm not sure we can say that anymore.

Say what?

Our boy.

I'm his mother. He'll always be my boy.

From what Hildy said to me this morning, I'm not sure that's true. She told me he doesn't want anything to do with us.

What's that supposed to mean?

It's not a confusing statement.

And you believe her?

Why wouldn't I? She knows him better than I do. Oh, and she did confirm that he's a real asshole. Apparently, he spends most of his time harassing people on the internet.

So what? Kids harass each other for fun all day. Look at how they treat each other on their phones. How could Atticus be worse than that?

Hildy says he's a troll and a bully. And we know he's a racist. Is that worse than being an asshole? Yeah, kinda. As for Francesca, well, I got the idea that, deep down, he didn't care about her or what she needed from him. He just took what he wanted when he wanted it. Seems like he treated Hildy that way too. And Petunia there. She almost died when he was supposed to be taking care of her.

She didn't look at me. She just traced rings of condensation with the bottom of the bottle.

And you know he can't really be 'ours' if he doesn't want to be, which it seems he doesn't. He could have asked me for help, couldn't he? He could have texted you, said, 'Mom, come help me. You know everybody who's anybody in this town—you can move mountains!'—But he didn't. Why? I'm thinking he must be truly angry with us. Not just family frustration mad. When we thought he was finally growing up, he was actually moving further away from us.

Did we fuck up?

Francesca and her friend think it had something to do with me.

Usually it's the mother who gets all the blame.

Your lucky day.

I wish I knew what exactly he was doing so we could tell him to stop.

Did Angel tell you how he treated the grips on his crew: losing their tools, breaking things, calling a day-player a gangbanger?

Fuck!

They refuse to work with him again.

I don't blame them.

By the way, I need to borrow some money to pay the guys for what he broke or lost.

Only if we split it fifty-fifty.

It's probably a grand. I thought Elizabeth had you working for nothing but options.

It's okay. Things are looking up. We've got a big announcement coming.

Can you get it in cash?

Sure. I'll bring it by tomorrow.

Great.

I dug at the beer label with my thumbnail.

Look, maybe I'm just one more father who doesn't want to accept responsibility for the way my kid behaves, but I don't think so. And not because I think it's your fault, but when I really consider what I, we, might have done to fuck him up, I keep coming up with nothing. And by nothing, I mean maybe it was the vacuum—the absence of a father who could be a role model. I'm not saying I would have been great or all that good, but I still would have been more than nothing. So, in the absence of another man saying don't treat women that way, don't treat dogs that way, don't treat any human like they owe you, like they're less than you, and feeling entitled to lose your shit when they don't agree with you, well, what do you get?

He was not some sort of out-of-control juvenile delinquent.

Of course, he wasn't, which is why he slipped by without our noticing. He was—and is—an entitled young white prick. And that's both my fault and not my fault, but whatever it is, it's not on you.

She took a long pull on the beer.

What do we do?

Wait him out. He's either gonna crash and burn or get his shit together—and whichever it is is pretty much beyond our control.

She didn't say anything. She just reached across the table for the bottle opener, opened another beer, and slid the opener through the rings of condensation back to me.

Twenties or fifties?

Doesn't matter. Call me when you have it—and maybe I can save you a trip to the Westside.

Wednesday, 7:00 p.m.

Normally, I'd take the 10 to the 110, exit on Hill and head south, but the traffic was so bad I had to take surface streets—Venice to Alvarado to Temple—so I came at Chinatown from an unfamiliar direction. Even so, I got to the restaurant twenty minutes early, parked across the street, sat in my car, and watched the door. I hadn't spent a lot of time in that part of Chinatown, and One China wasn't a restaurant I knew. I'd shot a bunch of times in the Central Plaza, which was a couple blocks north. Mostly action movies looking for "authentic" picture-postcard Los

Angeles to stage a fight or chase scene, but I never went down there if it wasn't for work. Chinatown didn't say Los Angeles to me. It was for tourists. Plus, the best Chinese food was in Monterey Park.

I was glad to see that there was lots of traffic on Ord Street and plenty of people passing on the sidewalk, but nobody went in or out of One China while I sat there.

Too many witnesses to get away with a murder, I thought.

I started to suspect that maybe One China was closed. Maybe Dr. Holly knew that—and maybe she was setting me up. Still, even if it was closed, what could I do? I mean so what if it didn't feel right, I had to take a chance.

At seven o'clock, I did what I was supposed to do: I crossed the street and opened the door. Two things I could see immediately that I had guessed wrong: the place wasn't closed, and it wasn't a trap. It was empty, just me, a couple of waiters leaning against a buffet in the back, and an old Chinese woman reading a paper at the hostess station.

Maybe the food's no good, I thought as I waited for the hostess to notice me. That would explain the lack of customers. Maybe Dr. Holly chose it so we could have some privacy.

I'd been standing there less than a minute when a group of Chinese men walked in and pushed past me. The hostess looked up at them, smiled, counted heads as she pulled out menus, and then led them to a table. It didn't exactly make me happy to have those guys jump the line, but I didn't think it would make that much of a difference. I could see plenty of empty two-tops, and besides, even though it was after seven, Dr. Holly hadn't arrived. I put my hand on the wooden podium as the hostess returned. Before I could even say party of two, she waved her hand in my face and said in a comically Hollywood stereotype, pronouncing her Rs like Ls

No loom.

I stopped myself from pointing over her shoulder.

We're only two.

No loom.

She stared emotionlessly at a spot behind me.

But those guys?

I pointed at the table of men who were laughing and drinking beer already.

They walked right in.

First come, first serve.

But I was here first, before them. I was standing here waiting when they walked in.

No leservation.

You don't know that. I'm meeting someone. She might have made a reservation.

No leservation. First come, first serve.

I was about to point out that she was contradicting herself when the door opened behind me, and two younger Chinese couples walked in. They were speaking English.

Any chance of a table for four? We're in kind of a hurry.

Absolutely. No problem, sir. We have plenty of room.

Suddenly, the Chinese hostess spoke perfect English.

I can seat you right away.

She showed them to a table in the middle of the room, listened to their objections, and then showed them to a more private table by the wall.

When she got back to her station, I was loaded for bear.

No loom

She said flatly in pidgin English—as if we hadn't just gone through this.

I can see you have plenty of tables. And I'm sure that the person I'm meeting must have made a reservation—

No leservation. First come, first serve.

That doesn't make any sense!

I slapped my hand on the hostess station. Nobody in the restaurant seemed to hear the noise.

Just check. It's Dr. Holly—

Before I could finish my complaint, someone grabbed my arm and yanked me into the dark. I found myself inches from Dr. Holly, her bottle lens glasses, and what smelled like a lifetime of unbrushed teeth. We were standing in a small alcove that was hidden from the reception area of the restaurant by floor-to-ceiling red velvet curtains. Off the left, I could see a long hallway that seemed to lead to bathrooms and storage and a door with an emergency exit light over it.

Shush!

She grabbed my shirt and pulled my face down to hers.

Stop complaining.

About what? I thought. Halitosis that could remove paint?

I tried not to inhale.

Did you hear what that hostess said? She's got a roomful of empty tables, and she keeps repeating: 'No loom, no loom.' What the fuck is going on here?

They don't serve Caucasians. Everybody knows that about One China.

That's illegal.

Maybe, but it is common knowledge. Caucasians are not welcome. DWP guys don't come here because they know they can't—

The door opened, and more people entered. She put her finger to her lips and kept it there until the hostess had seated them. Then she whispered

Why did Petunia send you to the lab like that? It was dangerous.

She didn't send me

I whispered back.

She knows to put the red flag in the flowerpot if she needs to talk to me.

Okay, well ... Dr. Holly ...

I didn't know how to give her the bad news.

My name is Dr. Martins. Dr. Holly Martins.

The combination of her breath and the insulting way she said this was enough to overcome my hesitation.

Petunia's dead, Dr. Martins.

She pressed her lips tightly together as her eyes grew six times wider behind her glasses. She didn't say anything; she just stared at me.

Breathe, I thought. Breathe!

I have the basket with the papers you gave her ... I mean, I'm only guessing that's what's in there since I haven't opened it completely. What I brought you I was able to fish out of the bottom.

She gulped.

How do you know Petunia's dead?

A couple of granny types from Blacks Only came to the house to tell me.

She was about to ask another question, but she closed her mouth and waited while the hostess seated more customers.

And you believed them?

Why wouldn't I? She was hit by a car on PCH. Apparently, she was high.

But you didn't see this with your own eyes. I mean, as far as you know, this is an unsubstantiated report. You did not personally witness her drug use.

Yes, I guess it is unsubstantiated.

I watched her consider this.

So, we don't have any factual proof that Ms. Biggars has been murdered or that she's even dead. The facts are, one, she brought the reports I gave her to you, two, you brought a copy of one of them to the lab and gave it to Dr. Lime, three, we arranged to meet at One China, and four, we have met. Can I assume you still have the original of the lab report?

I put it back in the basket.

Good.

She smiled and released a sigh of the undead.

I don't see any reason to change the plan.

What plan?

To make a movie and expose the criminal conspiracy.

What the fuck are you smoking? A movie based on what? Lab reports? Who came up with that?

Petunia, but I concurred with her analysis. Statistically, people love conspiracy movies.

A large party arrived, filling the small entrance hall, and pushing into the curtain. They seemed to be great friends of the hostess, and there was a lot of happy chatting in Chinese and big laughs before they were seated. I finally knew the reason Petunia had come to me, but I didn't know what facts she and the Nutty Professor wanted exposed.

What would the movie be about?

The DWP.

That's a grade-school documentary. What exactly at the DWP?

She was starting to explain when the door opened. Almost immediately, we felt the atmosphere change; whoever had just come in was not welcome. We both froze, intent upon hearing what was said, but no one was talking. The only sound was the periodic slurping through a straw of the last liquid in a cup. I was about to pull back the curtain to take a look when the hostess spoke.

No loom.

The Nutty Professor jumped.

There was a slurp, and then a man said,

We're meeting some friends here. They're probably already seated.

First come, first serve. No leservations.

Mind if my man and I look around for ourselves.

No loom.

Two Caucasian men looking for someone? I thought. My stomach turned over.

The Nutty Professor had heard enough. She reached inside her shirt and pulled out a chain with a small key on it. She unsnapped the key from the chain and pressed it into my palm.

Don't lose this. You'll need it for the movie

She mouthed the words.

What?

I mouthed back, but it was too late.

She was already tiptoeing cartoonishly down the hallway toward the exit. She slipped out the door and closed it without making a sound.

I briefly considered bluffing my way past the white guys but decided it was better to be safe than sorry and followed her. I found myself in a dark parking lot behind the restaurant and next to Velveteria: The Museum of Velvet Art. Unfortunately, it was closed. Otherwise, I would have ducked in there to hide. There was no sign of the Nutty Professor anywhere. I turned the key over in my right hand.

It had been an eventful day. The threats had become more threatening. According to the grannies, Petunia was dead, but Dr. Martins, for lack of a better word, her *development partner*, wasn't so sure. I didn't know who to believe. In any case, she didn't think it changed anything. Except, of course, it did since she clearly expected me to make a movie out of some lab reports she didn't have time to explain. I guess I could put a red flag in the flowerpot to arrange another meeting if I could find the right flowerpot. And then there was the key.

That's when I heard a woman scream in an alley directly across the parking lot from where I was standing. I ran toward it. Of course, the alley wasn't lit, and I couldn't see anything when I got closer. I stopped to listen and heard nothing unusual—no more screaming or life-or-death struggle—just the sounds of Chinatown at night. I knew it wasn't gonna be good enough to stand back and look in. Just like with the crawl space, I would have to go into the dark to check things out.

I pulled out my phone, turned on the flashlight, punched in 911, and put my thumb on send. Every step was tentative, but I made myself keep going, even when the alley turned darker and more twisted. The smell of rotten vegetables alternating with rancid grease made me nauseated on my empty stomach, but I didn't see anything alarming or suspicious—just a whole lot of rats and Chinese restaurant garbage.

When I reached what I later realized was the darkest part of the maze, I heard some car doors close and an engine turn over. Thinking I must be almost out, I hurried on until I emerged in another parking lot in time to see the back of a late model Maserati race away, straight toward the telltale glow of the 20K HMIs that meant a movie filming a night exterior. I took my finger off the send button as the recognition of a familiar world produced a warm glow in me. Sure, that was it: the movie explained the scream. Should I go check it out? See if I know anyone on the crew? Chances were good that I did, but no. The journey through the dark had taken too much out of me. Besides, I had to get home to the dog. I was struck by how good and responsible it made me feel to think of having Petunia at home waiting for me. I liked it.

I didn't see her until I reached my car. Her feet stuck out from under an overturned dumpster, twisted back on themselves like the feet of the Wicked Witch of the East. Forget ruby slippers—these low black heels were too scarred and broken down for anybody to get any magic out of them. I put my back into it, but I couldn't lift the dumpster off her body. It didn't matter. It was too late. She wasn't moving. Nothing I could do to help her. There was an eyeglass-shaped piece of half-inch-thick glass in a puddle of greasy water by my right foot.

I kicked it back under the dumpster. The Nutty Professor was dead.

Hard not to think she had the wrong facts about her partner too. Petunia was dead. You were asking about habeas corpus earlier? Well, you got your wish. Two down—and how many to go?

As far as I knew, just one. Yours truly.

Wednesday Later—and Then Too Late

Telling the truth to the cops turns out to take longer than you'd expect—even when they arrive on the scene only a couple of minutes after you find the body. And I did tell the truth, mostly, not because I wanted to, but because I knew my part from *The Maltese Falcon*: innocent guy mixed up in bad shit keeps his cool and comes out smelling like roses.

Yup, I knew her. No, not well. Dr. Martins. Holly Martins. Met her at the DWP this morning when I was researching a movie.

You'll notice I left out Lime and the reaction to the lab report. I didn't see the point of floating wacky conspiracy theories.

Yeah, that's right, I'm a screenwriter. Yes, the DWP. A romantic comedy actually. Title but no story. *Water Under the Bridge*? Sure, it's catchy, but there's more to a movie than a catchy title. I need a bridge to somewhere, right? Sure, she said she was interested in helping. No, just research, not casting. Asked me to meet her after work, for dinner. One China. Yes, really. Turns out we were the only two dimwits in town who didn't know that. Then what? Well, she'd changed her mind about helping, so it didn't matter about the Asian-only seating.

That was more me not connecting the dots for them than flat-out lying.

She'd changed her mind. Not very nice about it actually. No sorry for dragging me downtown in rush hour. She just left. I went to the bathroom and then walked out the back way. I'd seen a movie shoot in the plaza on my way in. Thought I'd walk over and see if I knew anyone. No, changed my mind. No, there's nothing going around. It was just too far to walk. And to tell the truth, I'd forgotten about my dog. How do you forget your dog? Easy, you don't have one your entire life. Very first day actually. A rescue from my daughter's clinic. So, I figured I better go make sure it hadn't destroyed the place. Funny story.

You know I can check all this out, right?

The detective said

It better add up is all I'm saying.

The Prius had idled down, but the car was in drive. Foot on the brake. The detective was leaning through the window and playing his part. Wannabe Dick Tracy. Bigfoot from *Inherent Vice*. *Muy pannacako* and cigarettes. So, I played mine. Smart-ass citizen.

You'll be able to add this one up on your fingers, Detective. One plus one equals two, remember?

She was alive when the dumpster landed on her, meaning she saw it coming, meaning it wasn't pleasant … in case you'd figured otherwise.

I hadn't.

He drew his weapon, standard-issue Glock 22 just like the Upgrades, and rested the butt on the top of the car door, a few inches from my shoulder.

You threatening me, Detective?

He didn't dignify the question.

More of a heads-up.

Inserting my index finger in the barrel, I rotated it away from my head toward the windshield.

I hope you're not expectin' a thank you.

Not really. I just have a hunch you know more than you're saying. And that the Charles Atlas who tipped that dumpster and turned that gal's head into marinara has the same hunch. Either that—or you're the one with all the muscles, which I doubt since you seem more like a Dolly Do-Gooder to me. That means, Agonistes, that you're between the devil and the deep blue sea—and both the devil and the sea are better armed than you'll ever be. And that means you're definitely in over your head.

Nothing I haven't heard before, Dick Tracy. Ask my daughter if you don't believe me.

That clearly wasn't what he'd expected me to say. He holstered his Glock then stroked his jaw like he was the real thing.

There won't be any good guy with the gun to save you when the bullets start flying. If that's what you're counting on.

Rest easy, Detective. I've made it a point in life to stay away from guns, and I have no intention of changing that.

That was the only time I lied.

I called Hildy as I drove up the ramp to the 101.

Hey, your brother come by to get his stuff yet?

Not that I know of, but it's possible.

So, it's still where we left it?

Probably.

I've been thinking I should hold on to it for him. Keep it safe.

I could almost hear her thinking.

If you're worried, honey, you can tell him you tried to stop me. I won't flip on you.

Whatever. When do you want to get it?

Now. Can you meet me?

No, but I'll call Ismael and tell him to let you in. Go to the emergency door in back.

Ismael?

Yeah, a new vet tech I hired. Full-fledged vet in Cuba, but he hasn't taken his tests here. He's covering the overnight shifts this week.

Has he met Atticus?

I just hired him yesterday.

Tell Ismael not to open the door for anyone but me.

I threw the phone onto the seat and punched the gas. It wasn't like I was late for anything, but then again, the way my night was going, I knew I was.

The parking lot out front was empty except for a broken-down beater next to the entrance. Hildy's clinic was dark. This didn't necessarily mean anything; it was eleven o'clock on a weeknight after all. I pulled around back and up next to the only door that had a light on over it; one of those metal fixtures that we used to say looked like a Chinaman's hat until we realized it was racist. I saw the emergency sign and a convenient parking place right in front of the door. Problem was the spot was sandwiched between two puke-green dumpsters. Not a good omen. I backed the car up, kept the engine running, and flashed the building with my brights. I didn't catch anyone lurking in the shadows, but I couldn't think my way out of the anxiety twisting up my gut.

What were the chances Atticus was in there now? Next to zero, right? If he had wanted the gun, he would have already gotten it. And he wouldn't have left it behind in the first place if it were that important to him. Chances were he'd forgotten he even had it. Besides, what did he need a gun for? He might have a lot of rage, but he hadn't tried to kill anyone—or threatened to—that I knew of anyway.

I turned off the engine, sat in the dark, and waited for the rats to come out. They didn't. I gave myself some second thoughts: maybe it wasn't a gun I'd felt. I hadn't seen it, had I? Probably one of those vape things. For pot. Still better to be sure.

I got out of the car, shut the door quietly, and headed for the emergency entrance. That's when I heard a gunshot. I froze. It came from inside the clinic.

So, Detective Tracy, how does the good guy without a gun stop the bad guy now?

I projected my question into outer space and then decided it wasn't a bad guy. It was Atticus.

The door had been pried open. I didn't like that.

Ismael?

I figured it was safer to announce myself than surprise him.

It's Hildy's dad, Sam.

The corridor was dark, but I could see a band of light at the bottom of the door into the overnight ward down at the end. No one answered, but I kept up the pretense as I walked toward the light.

Hildy was supposed to call you to tell you I was coming by to pick up some medicine for my dog.

I took a breath and slowly pushed the door open into the overnight ward.

Ismael?

There was no sign of him or Atticus until the door was all the way open—and I found myself staring into the barrel of a gun for the second time in the space of an hour. This one was pointed at me by my son. He was grinning—and too far away for me to grab.

Hey, son

I said

What's going on? Where's Ismael?

He nodded toward the wall of cages but didn't say anything.

You're not planning on shooting me, are you?

His grin broadened.

I'm not planning anything. We're playing a game.

We?

Me and the mutts.

These dogs?

And the illegal. He's a mutt too.

He reached up, spun the revolver quickly, pointed the gun at a cage, and fired. I heard a dog yelp and saw blood spatter on the wall.

Fuck!

He had the gun on me again.

Immigrants aren't mutts, son.

Dregs, scum, lowest of the low, call them whatever you want. They're all rapists and freeloaders. That's why they're in cages.

I noticed a man's limp hand on the floor of Petunia's old cage.

Ismael? Hey, Ismael! Are you okay? What the fuck, son? Did you shoot Ismael?

I took a step toward the cage. Atticus fired, splintering the doorframe by my head and stopping me.

What the fuck are you doing?

Playing Russian roulette, Dad. You can watch as long as you don't get in the way.

He swung the revolver off of me, pulled the trigger, shot another dog, and then swung it back on me.

Isn't this fun?

Not really.

He shrugged me off, spun the revolver, quickly aimed at another cage, and pulled the trigger. Nothing.

Shit!

He spun the revolver again and aimed at the cage with Ismael.

Stop!

Why?

He pointed the gun at me again.

Because you're not playing it right. First of all, you've got too many bullets in there.

What do you mean? There's empties. You saw me spin it.

Okay, well, then it's your turn.

Fuck off!

Sure, it is. In Russian roulette, everybody has to put his life on the line. It's not just one guy standing in the middle of the room taking turns shooting people. You've shot four times that I know of, and I can see you've already shot at Ismael once. That means it's your turn.

That got to him, and his grin faded.

Maybe a good guy without a gun could save the day.

But heck, there's no reason you have to keep playing. Looks like you've had plenty of fun already.

Atticus shook his head.

Okay, so I'm not playing Russian roulette then. My game is American roulette. And the way you play my game is that a patriotic American loads five rounds into his revolver, spins and shoots, spins and shoots, till he runs out of bullets.

That doesn't seem fair.

Fuck fair. Is it fair all these criminals running loose in our country and taking what doesn't belong to them? Who said just because rag-head illegals have it rough back home that they're entitled to ours?

Ismael isn't a rag head, and he isn't illegal, Peck. He's Cuban. And he's a doctor,

Hildy said from the corridor behind me.

Stay where you are, honey. Your brother's got a gun.

She didn't listen to me. She was standing in the open door.

I have his paperwork right here. Put the gun down, and I'll show you.

Fuck that. Every illegal has paperwork. Paperwork doesn't make you an American.

I don't think the cops will agree with you.

Cops?

I thought I saw a flicker of doubt.

Yeah, the cops. I called them from the parking lot a minute ago.

Atticus's grin flashed back to life.

The cops will see I'm doing a public service. I'm the real Atticus. Not some fictional pantywaist.

He giggled.

I'll make sure justice prevails.

He reached up and spun the revolver again.

My turn!

I shouted and stopped him from shifting his aim.

He shook his head.

I said you could watch—not that you could play.

Why not?

Because the odds are already against white people in this country. We can't shoot each other.

But I like my white guy odds. If you're telling the truth, and you only loaded five, there's only one round left in that gun. Give me the gun—and I'll do it if you're too scared.

Fuck you, Dad. I'm not that stupid.

He shook his head and laughed, half closing his eyes at the ridiculousness of what I was suggesting.

I ducked under the barrel of the gun and charged, tackling him and driving him back into the cot, which snapped up around us like the jaws of a great white.

The gun went off, Hildy piled on, and we wrestled on the floor. It ended with me sitting on Atticus's head and Hildy sitting on his chest until the cops swarmed in.

Tell him you love him, Dad

Hildy said as they dragged Atticus away.

But I didn't. How could I? It was too late for words. For Atticus. And for two of the dogs, but thankfully not for Ismael. He'd been hit in the shoulder and lost a lot of blood, but the EMTs thought he would make it.

What's that on your head, Dad?

Hildy reached up and ran her fingers across my scalp.

It looks like you burned yourself with a curling iron.

She pulled her hand away.

You're bleeding.

I reached up and touched it.

It's nothing. Maybe the leg of the cot hit me.

Hildy shook her head.

That's a near miss, Dad.

She looked at the blood on her fingertips. She seemed shocked, like she couldn't process it.

Peck almost blew your brains out.

I wiped my fingers on my pants and shrugged. No point in correcting her. What was I gonna say? Doesn't feel like "almost" to me?

Thursday, Darkest before the Dawn

Petunia hadn't moved off her bed, and I couldn't convince her she needed to. I probably should have insisted, but I didn't have it in me. I leaned down and whispered into her cone

Fuck it. Pee in the house if you want to—just don't tell my Ex or Hildy.

I sat on the couch and took long pulls at the bottle of Herradura. It may not have been a good idea to get drunk, but I figured I wouldn't be able to sleep with all the chaos and misery swirling in my head. More violence in the past twenty-four hours than my whole life put together. Real violence that is. Movie violence I could handle plenty of, but images of the Nutty Professor's twisted feet, Ismael's bloody hand, those butchered dogs, and my son off his fuckin' rocker were running on a loop in my head. Blood everywhere, and if Detective Bigfoot Tracy was right, more coming. Probably mine.

I took the key the Nutty Professor gave me out of my pocket and squinted at it. No question it fit the basket padlock, but digging into that treasure trove would have to wait.

I had to figure out about a lawyer for Atticus and how I could scrounge up bail. Might be pretty high. 'Course, maybe he should stay behind bars. Safer for him and everyone involved, but I wonder how his mom and sister would feel about that. He hadn't killed anyone after all. How many years can you get for putting someone in a cage and shooting at them? Probably a whole lot.

Even in my degraded condition, I knew nothing was going to be decided in the dark. I had to get some sleep, but it was too damn hot in my house to sleep. So, I got naked again, polished off the tequila, and tried to stop debating whether I should let my kid face the music without me by his side.

You might be amazed to hear that I was passed out on the couch when the crash came. When you reckon on the danger and how it all turned out, it seems crazy that a sane man could spend most of an entire week—maybe the most important of his life—naked and/or unconscious, but that's the way it was.

What the fuck?

I shouted, but I thought I knew what was actually the fuck and my subconscious was screaming,

Yours truly! Yours truly!

But that same subconscious also remembered that there was a monster raccoon stalking me. I took a breath, calmed down, and tried to figure out what exactly was up.

That was when I noticed that the dog wasn't on her bed. Whew! It wasn't the deep state from the DWP coming for me, and it wasn't my nemesis; it was the dog doing nighttime dog things. She finally decided she wants to get up, and she's knocked something over. Even though I'd told her she could pee in my house, I jumped up to get her out the kitchen door open and correct that misstatement. She wasn't in the kitchen. I ran to my bedroom—not there. Hildy's room? Not there either. Fuck! Where was the dog? So even though I didn't expect she'd heard her name enough to know it, I shouted into the dark.

Petunia?

Imagine how surprised I was to hear a response:

Yeah?

The voice was tentative and weak, and although female, not a dog's. It seemed to be coming from the bathroom. I pushed open the door and discovered Petunia the dog with her white plastic cone staring at an unknown mass tangled up in my shower curtain. I say unknown, but that wasn't true exactly. It was more like yet to be positively identified, but it didn't take a PhD to figure out that the Nutty Professor had been right. The grannies had given me bad intel. Petunia Biggars hadn't been run over on the PCH—unless you wanted to believe she'd been resurrected in my bathtub. It also didn't take a genius to realize that resurrected or never dead, she was back on the hit list. I triaged the situation.

God damn it, Petunia, I thought you were housebroken.

The human Petunia did not like being associated with the word *housebroken*.

She hissed at me.

What the fuck is your problem, old man?

I waved my hands to get her shut up. The dog Petunia gave a helpful bark to second my injunction.

Why didn't you wake me up instead of crapping on the floor?

Are you actually saying that I'm not civilized enough to use a toilet?

The human Petunia raised her voice enough to panic me.

I threw myself on top of her and clamped my hand over her mouth.

Shut the fuck up!

I turned my head and shouted toward the living room.

Are you actually pissing right in front of me, Petunia?

Listen, man!

The human Petunia was mad; she was shouting into my hand and punching me in the ribs. I held on for dear life.

She shouted

If you think I'm gonna let some perverted, naked white guy …

I shouted louder

If you think I'm gonna let some geriatric rescue ...

She lowered her voice slightly

Hump me in his bathtub.

I shouted

Take dumps in my bathroom.

Then I jammed my mouth in her ear.

Shut the fuck up! You're going to get us both killed.

She bit my hand.

I jerked it out of her mouth and shook it as she pushed me off of her. Thankfully, I could see that she'd finally understood. I gestured for her to stay put and then turned to the dog.

All right, Petunia, it's the backyard for you.

I took the dog by the cone and, talking to her all the way, pulled her along through the house, first to the alarm pad and then out the kitchen door.

We're gonna have to come up with a need-to-go signal pretty fast. I can't have you crapping or pissing in the house. That's a deal-breaker. So, give me little warning in the future. I know you can do it. I heard a little bark in there. Don't think I didn't.

By the time I'd finished my lecture, we were standing in the backyard.

Okay, now put whatever you've got in you out here from now on.

Petunia the dog obliged me by squatting and peeing.

Great

I said too loudly for that time of night

Let's look at this as a learning opportunity. You can go back to bed now.

She did not. She waddled around and sniffed the ground.

Okay, round two. Get it all out.

I looked back at the window into the bathroom.

The human Petunia had jimmied it open and climbed through. I didn't like how easy it had been to get in the house or the fact that the alarm didn't go off, but at the moment, I was glad to see that the window wasn't broken. We could close it, and no one would be the wiser.

My eyes drifted to the satellite dish on the roof. What the fuck was I going to do about the cameras and the mics? Maybe the Upgrades had bought my sideshow for now but even if there weren't cameras in the bathroom, the human Petunia couldn't stay in there forever; and not just for her sake. It was my only bathroom and I liked to think I was housebroken. If Petunia thought having me lie on top of her was bad, wait till she sat through one of my bowel movements. I could crawl under the house and pull out that box or just cut the cable, but then they'd know that I was on to them. Better if I could fuck with the signal somehow, but how? Then it occurred to me. Malicious raccoons attack cables! Leave the box where it was. Act II of my little make-believe with Petunia. As I was crossing the yard to get my ladder, I narrated the action

Look at that, Petunia, those goddamn raccoons are up there on the roof next to the dish. How about you scare them off before they fuck up my TV again?

It must have been quite a sight: me crawling naked across my roof to the dish, ripping out the satellite cables, and chewing on them to make bite marks, all while my dog's looking up at me like I'm insane.

I'm scared of those fuckers, you know? They're mean, and they're not scared of anything, man or dog. How many times have they done this chewing through the cable just to fuck with me? What is it with vermin and electrical cables? It's not like it's food.

Petunia got bored and went back inside before I finished. I found her in the bathroom with her conehead bumping against the tub and the human Petunia patting her head with all the enthusiasm of someone who doesn't like dogs. I wrapped a towel around my waist, closed the door, and turned on the water in the sink.

The room was crowded and smelled like unwashed dog. I put the seat down on the toilet, sat down, and leaned over to talk to the human Petunia.

Sorry about that

I whispered and made vague gestures to indicate what I meant about being on top of her.

It's all right, I guess.

She tried to push the cone away from her.

Petunia, the dog, pushed back.

I should have figured they'd found you. That they wouldn't stake you out when they could just bug the place. It just fucked with my head to have an old white man pinning me down. I hope I haven't screwed things up completely.

We'll have to wait and see.

Shouldn't we make a run for it?

I'm thinking that we're safer here. I mean, if they thought they had caught you, they'd have been in here before I managed to shut you up.

So, you're hoping they'll buy two animal stories for the price of one: first the incontinent dog and then the maniacal raccoon?

I shrugged.

But you're still whispering.

Better safe than sorry, I think, till we know we're out of the woods.

How will we know?

I'm not sure exactly, but there will be something. Until then, we should assume that we're still being watched. I may not have actually disabled their devices by pulling out the cables.

So, what then, me imprisoned in a bathtub?

I'm afraid so. I can get you some pillows and blankets.

I guess that's better than sleeping under a tarp in a homeless camp off PCH.

You know, some church ladies told me that you were dead.

Good. That's what I told them to say.

Why the fuck would you do that?

To scare you a little. Fuck with your head. Give you a taste of what life is like for people of color.

How is that exactly?

Walking around knowing that even if you haven't done anything wrong, someone's out to get you.

I don't see the point of knowing that in this situation. It didn't help Dr. Martins.

What's that supposed to mean?

She knew they were out to get her, and they still got her.

Oh shit, no!

She put her hand over her mouth.

What happened?

They trapped her in an alley and killed her. I found her under a dumpster.

Excuse me? What the fuck were you doing there? And how do you even know who she is?

Petunia was suddenly very angry—as if I were responsible for the Nutty Professor's murder.

Why didn't you stay the fuck out of it? I told you to drop the white savior crap.

Why?

I had a hard time keeping my voice down.

Why? Because you didn't let me. First, you show up at my door, then you leave your bike, then you send the church ladies to tell me you're dead and that I should carry on your work. I don't know what you have to be angry about. I didn't kill her—and you're the one who lied to me.

She retreated.

Okay, sorry. Look, clearly, I'm not dead. And I'm sorry if what I said was too much. I just wanted to warn you and make sure you were looking after my bike. You have it, right? You didn't let those guys take it from you.

It's in the living room. I hid it under a bunch of clothes and shit. It's all there. If you don't believe me, I can bring you the stuff from the basket.

She didn't like this information.

How would you do that? It's locked up.

I have a key.

Her brow wrinkled and then relaxed.

I think you have a lot of explaining to do, Samson, but it's going to have to wait. You've been in this bathroom way too long if they're still watching.

Shall I get you some blankets and pillows?

It would be nice, but, no. Nothing unusual happens in this house until we're in the clear.

Okay … well, there are these.

I stood up, pulled a bunch of used towels and clothes off the back of the door, and handed them to her.

Sorry if those are a little crusty. I don't do my laundry that often.

I'll survive.

I looked down at her.

I'm glad you're alive.

Thanks.

Her expression shifted. She looked at the dog.

Why is your dog named Petunia?

I hadn't planned on ever having this conversation, so I wasn't ready with an answer.

She's a rescue.

And that was her name when you got her?

I couldn't lie.

She was abandoned and tied to a post in Hancock Park, so, no, she didn't have a name.

The human Petunia considered this.

And when exactly did you rescue this dog?

This morning.

I'm not sure how I feel about this.

I finally said what was obvious.

I didn't expect I'd ever see you again.

So, for some weird reason, you named a shelter dog after me?

Yes.

She reached out and patted the dog tentatively on the head.

Okay, well, we'll talk.

Thursday, 7:00-ish a.m.

I sat up the rest of the night waiting for the Upgrades to do something. I was pretty sure biting through the cables had cut off their surveillance. It was only a matter of time before they would react—send someone to restore the connection, bounce sonic waves through the walls to explode our heads, send bug-sized drones down the chimney. I was actually surprised they went so low tech in the end.

I was sitting on a chair in the middle of the living room, back in a version of my "gripster" uniform as Ja'K called it—no shirt, unhooked Carrhart overalls. It was too hot and airless to be wearing clothes, but I didn't want to upset the human Petunia any more than I already had. She remained in the bathroom with the door open so she could get a little air. Now and then, I'd hear the sound of her flopping around trying to get comfortable. The dog Petunia was on her bed, snoring.

It was pretty early in the morning. Not dawn. Later. That moment when there's no more dark to disappear, but most people are still in bed. They pulled in quietly: two Suburbans up onto my lawn. There weren't any revving motors, screeching brakes, or slamming car doors—just masses flickering like a black-and-white movie through the gaps in my blinds and a slight increase in the density of the atmosphere like when too many people crowd into a room. Then came pounding.

Police! Open up! Open up! Police!

Out of the woods and into the frying pan, I thought.

Forget the formalities, they were coming in. It was only a matter of whether I could delay them long enough for Petunia to run for it. The entire front of my teardown shack seemed to be listing toward me as I slowly walked to the door.

Hold on. I'm not decent

I shouted my stock line. The pounding stopped, but I continued shouting loud enough so that Petunia would hear me.

One second, one second. I'm hooking my overalls.

I was actually struggling to get a hold of the straps without letting go of the bib. The bathroom door slammed shut.

Stand aside! Or face the battering ram!

I did not stand aside. I just gave up on the straps, hoisted up my overalls under my armpits, and opened the door before they could break it down. I half expected one of those cartoon moments with six guys holding the ram torpedoing in my front door through the house and out the back. But there was no battering ram, just the Upgrades rushing me like defensive ends after the quarterback. I blocked them the best I could, but my overalls dropping into a tangle around my ankles didn't make that easy. That was when I heard the kitchen door burst open and the pounding of boots behind me.

There was no rear escape route; the Upgrades were on all sides. I stepped out of the way and made a show of pulling my overalls up and getting decent. The Upgrades searched the house methodically. I could hear them opening closets and lifting furniture. They hadn't reached the bathroom yet, but they would soon enough.

I found my phone and tried to think of someone to call: my Ex, Angel, Hildy. I wondered for a bit what the chances were that Atticus and I could get a two-for-one discount on a lawyer or if maybe I could arrange for us to share the same prison cell if we both pled guilty.

One of the Upgrades saw my bicycle art project in the living room and started jumping up and down. He was windmilling his clone to join him as he started pulling clothes off it. Seems I had underestimated Cleft and No-Cleft. They did know what they were looking for.

Jackpot, Ashton!

Ashton, the one with the cleft chin, hurried over and pitched in, digging through my discards till he found the basket. When he did, the two grabbed it simultaneously, pulling first one way and then the other, fighting like kids over a toy on the playground, but the chain held. The basket stayed attached to the bike, and the basket did not open.

Let's take the whole bike

No-Cleft suggested.

We don't have a bike rack.

It'll fit in the back.

You think?

Hold on, fellas, you talking about stealing my daughter's bike?

I put my hand on the seat. Ashton ignored my accusation and lifted the lock.

Where's the key, Samson?

Even if these two had killed the Nutty Professor, something about the clownishness of the Upgrades in a tug-of-war over national secrets switched me back to offense.

Where's your warrant?

You're in possession of stolen national secrets; a warrant won't save you. Give us the key

Ashton said.

Not me, Ashton. You. You're the one who needs the warrant. Otherwise, this whole search and seizure's inadmissible.

No-Cleft ignored me.

You're a traitor to your country, Agonistes. You're going up the river for the rest of your life.

I expressed some genuine confusion.

Tell me why, if I'm a traitor, and you didn't bring a warrant, I would give you the key?

The logic of this seemed to fry their brains. They went ballistic, taking their frustration out on the bike and the basket. Ashton clawed at the lid, while No-Cleft tried to use his car keys to saw at the leather straps. The harder they struggled, the more I was convinced that whatever the deep state was up to, they were basically still bozos which meant the odds were evening up in this showdown—odds but not the numbers. Man to man to woman, the Upgrades outnumbered us.

Then, behind me, the search party arrived at the bathroom door. I held my breath as they leaned into it, pushing as if they were meeting resistance.

Fuck, I thought. Petunia did not get away. We're dead meat.

I was wrong. Because it wasn't the human Petunia that was waiting for them; it was conehead Petunia, my unexpectedly ferocious, barking, snarling, biting, fucking terrifying rescue German shepherd lunging for and scaring the shit out of the adjunct Upgrades who were falling all over themselves to get away.

Petunia inspired me to launch my own counterattack; mustering all the old middle linebacker Samson I could manage, I slammed my forearms into Ashton and No-Cleft, separating them from the bike and basket and sending them flying across the living room.

They were shocked but not too shocked to shout more threats as they scrambled back to their feet.

This isn't gonna look good for you, Samson! You're going down!

Get the fuck out of my house!

On my right flank, Petunia raged down the hallway toward the door, barking and growling, snapping and biting, slicing ankles and Achilles with her plastic cone, generally scattering whoever strayed into her path.

As the adjunct Upgrades ran past, I took my own best shots, hurling myself into one and then the other, chest bumping them out of my house. I slammed the door behind them and threw the bolt.

And just like that, almost unbelievably, the home invasion was over. We had survived. Like it had never happened. Petunia looked up at me from out of her cone, rolled her eyes as if to say she'd seen worse, and went back to her bed. She wasn't even panting.

You can come out now!

I gave the all clear. I heard the bathroom door burst open, a rush of bare feet down the hallway, a sudden stop, a return to the bathroom, and then a new path through the dining room. The human was giving the dog a wide berth.

Are they gone?

Not completely. I can see them sitting in their Suburban.

But you think it's safe for me to come out? Ow!

Petunia cried out and jumped sideways. The dog had followed her to the window and sliced her Achilles with the edge of the cone. Petunia hopped away. The dog stayed on her heels, trapping her in the corner.

The cameras are definitely down, so as long as we stay out of sight, yes, we're safe.

As long as we have her

She added, rubbing the wound on her foot.

Thanks, Petunia.

She put her other hand on the top edge of the cone to stop the dog's advance on her.

Now how do I get her to leave me alone?

How should I know? I only got her yesterday.

Well, can you at least get her off me please?

I called the dog, but she only pushed harder on her namesake.

The way she's acting is kind of a compliment; she never got out of bed before you crashed the party.

That's great, and I feel really special, but just so you know, I'm scared of dogs.

Even one that has saved your life?

No doubt she was incredible, but she didn't save my life. Those clowns aren't the ones trying to kill me. The guys after me are from the government.

Petunia used her free hand to pull the blinds back enough to peer out.

They look like killers to you? They're sitting there playing with their phones. One of them keeps swiping left like he's on Tinder. Nope, those guys are from the DWP.

I thought public utilities were the government.

Even as I said this, I realized I sounded pretty stupid. Petunia shook her head dismissively.

It depends. Some are more government-like than others. The LADWP is a municipal utility; they sent those guys to recover their secrets, but they don't have the balls to kill me.

But they're armed.

Think about it, those clowns—and they are clowns—were run off by a dog. If they were real baddies, they would have just shot her.

So, if those guys are from the DWP, where are the guys who are trying to kill you?

Everywhere.

Everywhere?

Turn over any rock.

Do they know you're here?

It wouldn't surprise me.

I turned away from the window. I was confused.

Can you explain to me the connection between the DWP sending the clown patrol to get back their secrets and some unseen government forces trying to kill you? How's that work exactly?

I don't know *exactly*.

She made air quotes.

Give me your best guess.

It'll sound like some kind of crazy made-up conspiracy.

Try me.

Okay, we all know what the FBI did to King and Malcolm X. Those are facts, but those two were just the tip of the iceberg. All the civil rights leaders were harassed by the government. And even though it was the FBI who took the fall, think about what was happening, what they were trying to suppress: an entire race. One agency isn't enough for that. It takes the whole goddamn apparatus. Look at who was excluded from the original Social Security Act in 1935: agricultural and domestic workers, half of the US economy at the time and mostly African American. Look at the housing act from the year before—that's where redlining started.

What's redlining again?

She seemed exasperated by how little I knew about my country's history.

It means denying mortgages to people living in certain areas—basically keeping black people from accumulating wealth through property ownership.

Oh, right, I remember

I pretended.

Go on. Where's the conspiracy?

In every branch of government: Congress, the courts, the White House, the FBI, CIA, and NSA. Fast-forward to today and what's happening. Everywhere you look, the police are getting away with killing African Americans. Nothing's happening to those guys, but what's happening to the people who are protesting: the activists, the musicians, the artists?

I don't know.

They're dying under mysterious circumstances. Freak car accidents, make-no-sense assaults, supposed suicides, overdoses when they've never done drugs, and fatal health problems that pop up out of nowhere.

It did sound like a pretty wild-assed conspiracy theory, but then the image of the crushed Nutty Professor flashed before my eyes.

I guess that explains Dr. Martins. I thought it was the DWP, but I never saw her killers.

That doesn't surprise me. So, what exactly happened?

She told me to meet her in a restaurant in Chinatown. I did. Unfortunately, some creepy guys came in and scared her off before she told me that much. She did give me the key. On my way back to my car, I found her under a dumpster.

What creepy guys? What did they look like?

I didn't see them. They were on the other side of a thick curtain.

Okay. That explains how you have a key to my basket, but it doesn't explain why *exactly* you involved yourself in the first place.

She seemed skeptical.

I gave her a quick rundown of my day, starting with Beach Ball and Toothpick and ending with passing out on the couch. I didn't skip over playing American roulette with my son, but I didn't make too big a deal of it. She seemed less angry when she heard how I happened to be in Chinatown, but it was also clear she hadn't entirely forgiven me for messing around in her shit. It all came down to whether or not the church ladies had told me they had saved me so that I could carry on Petunia's work.

Why would they say that? Leave you to fill in the blanks when they knew I was alive? As if *you* could replace *me*.

I don't know why they said it. You were sleeping under a tarp, remember?

She gave a dismissive snort, which really irked me. I had had it.

Look, I filled in the blanks as best I could. You wish I hadn't. Standard game of telephone. What really matters is if we can now work together to save both our lives.

She didn't have an answer. Then Petunia swiped her with the cone again. She shrieked,

God damn it! Get away from me, dog!

She climbed up on her bike and put her feet on the handlebars.

Petunia sat down by the front tire and looked at her. The cone scraped, scraped, scraped against the rubber as the dog panted and stared up at Petunia. Petunia looked at me. I shrugged my shoulders.

Okay

I said

Fill in the blanks the way you want. Let's start with the easy one. What did Dr. Martins give you that is so top secret they killed her for it?

She hesitated but not long enough to get me mad.

The stuff in my basket.

Of course, but what is that stuff? Dr. Martins said something about you two trying to develop a movie from it. All I saw was a lab report. Bunch of numbers that didn't make a lot of sense to me.

Another silence. Then a juke followed by an embarrassed smile.

Would you mind if I took a shower?

I nodded okay and only then noticed what she was wearing.

Why are you grinning like an idiot? That was not an invitation.

'Course not. 'Course not.

What is it then? We don't stand a chance if you're half goofy.

She was right. I was going goofy, but for good reason. I had just noticed that she was wearing an old piece of my movie swag. It was an oversized megaplush terry cloth bathrobe with "Samson" embroidered in big gold letters across the back, a wrap gift from this campy chick flick, *Femme Fatal*, I'd worked on a few years back. That was the working title, I don't know if they ever released it, referred to some kind of expensive cream that was poisoning spoiled rich women. The movie took place at a high-end spa in Napa. The A-list actresses pooled their per diem and gave everyone on the crew these superexpensive robes. I don't normally wear robes—it seems like kind of a useless middle step between nothing and what you're supposed to be wearing—so I'd given it to Hildy. And she'd loved it, and worn it, practically her second skin, till she took it off for good.

That's my daughter's robe. I'm smiling because I'd forgotten about it.

But it's got your name on the back.

Once upon a time, that was her favorite thing about it— after how soft it was.

Petunia hugged herself.

It's very soft and snuggly. Is it okay if I borrow it?

Why not? Hildy doesn't want it. And I'd forgotten it. I say it's finders keepers.

Thanks. Now maybe you could pull this dog off me long enough for me to get to the bathroom.

I grabbed the cone and led Petunia back toward her bed.

And one more thing

She was running down the hall

If we're gonna have any future, your junk can't be putting in appearances. You let a naked man parade around in front of you, and he pretty quick gets the idea that you like what you see and you've invited him to party.

I laughed as she closed and locked the bathroom door.

While she was in the shower, I pulled all the food out of the refrigerator and the cupboards and laid it out on the kitchen counter. It was good to take inventory see how long we could hold out; my Ex hadn't exactly stocked the shelves. I would have to go shopping soon.

When Petunia was done with her shower, I pointed her into Hildy's room.

Make yourself comfortable in there. If there are clothes you like, take them. All the food in the house is on the kitchen counter. I'm going to get myself cleaned up too. Oh, and here's your key back.

I held it out for her.

She looked at it for minute without taking it, so I put it on the table and left her standing in the doorway taking in my daughter's teenage life.

By the time I was bathed and shaved and dressed more like a writer than a grip, she was sorting piles of papers on my dining room table and devouring a sandwich. The dog was under the table with her cone between Petunia's legs.

I hoped this meant they'd made their peace. She was still wearing the Samson robe over a pair of Hildy's shorts and a *Manifest Destiny* T-shirt.

Find what you wanted?

It's all here

She was talking with her mouth full and waving a greasy hand at the papers.

I meant to eat.

She made a face as if to say no, but she would work with it.

What is all this?

I glanced at the papers and saw what looked like printed-out emails and memos with the DWP letterhead. She put her sandwich on the table.

All this is proof of a conspiracy at the DWP that's worse than their draining of the Owens Lake and the rape of that watershed.

Really? What's it prove?

When you put all the pieces of the puzzle together, it's crystal clear that the DWP has been conducting illegal experiments on the black population of Los Angeles.

Shit.

They've been mixing gray water in with POC's normal water to cut down the consumption for the entire city and thereby reach the state-mandated reductions.

Gray water? Like water from showers or dishwashers?

Like water that used to get treated in sewage plants and then flushed out into the bay. Some of that gray water is now being redirected through an additional chemical process before being mixed into the drinking water going to homes in Compton and Watts and Monterey Park—wherever there's a high concentration of undesirables. Besides a usage scam, it's a huge fucking experiment to figure out if humans can drink recycled water. And it's being tested out only on POCs, just like the Tuskegee syphilis experiments. The DWP targets people of color for a program that is advertised as a citywide pilot conservation program. They think they're getting free water in exchange for participating in a study, but what they're actually getting is all the crap that the citizens of Los Angeles put down their drains that no amount of processing or filtering will ever get out: drugs, chemicals, viruses, bacteria, what have you.

I scanned the papers and tried to get my mind around this.

Just so I get it straight, you're saying there's some kind of conspiracy at the DWP to make minorities the test subjects in a secret water conservation experiment?

Her mouth was full of sandwich, and she just nodded enthusiastically. I picked up one of the stacks and leafed through it to give myself some time to think. She talked with her mouth full, pointing at one pile and then another.

Emails, lab reports for the program, and then memos from the cover-up. The evidence is all right here once you understand the code. Dr. Martins was our whistle-blower.

Okay, well, I'm mostly a skeptic when it comes to grand conspiracies that require a lot of people to cooperate.

You would think differently if you were black.

Sure, if I were black, I would expect to be getting the short end if I even got the stick. Still, I don't really see what the point of mixing gray water into the drinking water of African Americans would be—even as an experiment. What's the end game? I don't know what Tuskegee is, sorry, but I do know that when all is said and done, the DWP could never turn around and say we figured out this great way to recycle and reuse water. Let's all start doing it. 'Cause sooner or later, someone's going ask, 'How do you know it won't make people sick—or kill them?' And what are they gonna say? 'We've tested it out on African Americans.' No fucking way. Not in today's world.

As Petunia listened to my debunking, she smiled and shook her head.

Okay, you admit you don't know much about the history of POCs and government, but wait till you hear the whole thing before you get so know-it-all on me.

Okay.

Answer me this: what is the one surefire way for humanity to conserve water?

Use less.

She shook her head again.

That's a method, but it's not guaranteed. Look at those assholes in Bel Air who were watering their lawns and running their fountains during the last drought. No, the only surefire way to reduce water consumption is for there to be fewer people.

Okay.

We need to reduce the population in Los Angeles and in America too, and we all know that there are ways to incentivize people to have fewer babies: birth control, etcetera. Now stay with me. Assume that the powers that be want fewer people in order to conserve natural resources, but fewer people to the powers that be doesn't mean fewer white people. It means fewer undesirable people: Latinx immigrants, Asians, and blacks. They've as much as announced they want this country to stay majority white, right?

Okay.

The real government experiment is not if you can survive drinking gray water. The real experiment is how to reduce the population of blacks and immigrants without anyone knowing it. You can't propagandize a whole lot of racist policies on TV and billboards. You can't be that obvious. I mean, the reason no one's accused the cigarette companies of racism is because their ads aren't out-and-out racist; they're just advertising to blacks in their communities. Free market's not racist, right? It's predatory, but it doesn't look racist because the message is the same no matter who you are: smoke. Then why aren't there any ads in white neighborhoods? They don't have an answer, but *free markets* is how they get away with it. Now when it's basically gray water eugenics we're talking about, you have to have a conspiracy. You can't have billboards in Compton telling poor people to get an abortion, you'll like it, or if you stop having babies, you can get a new car, or here, have some free birth control. You can't have ads like that in one place and nothing in West LA or Simi Valley.

They needed to figure out something that works without anyone knowing, some secret way to get all black women to be on birth control without knowing they're on birth control. Which means you not only have to have access to a consistent drug-delivery system, but you need an unlimited quantity of the drugs themselves. And you don't want to involve the drug manufacturers 'cause then you either have to pay for it or explain what you're up to. Where's the largest stockpile of birth control drugs in the world?

I don't know. China?

No. In the wastewater from American toilets and swimming pools. All those rich white women who can afford family planning are pissing their birth control into the sewers and out into the ocean. So, all the man's gotta do is take that stream of chemicals, clean it up enough so it doesn't stink, and send it down the pipes and into the drinking water of the black women he's trying to render infertile.

It was a little too sci-fi for me.

How could that even work? I mean, how could there be enough birth control medication concentrated in the water to prevent pregnancies. It would be too diluted. Besides, there's all that other medicine in there as well: antidepressants, Viagra, Cialis, ibuprofen, aspirin, and not to mention the household crap and soaps.

There's no question that there's a lot of bad shit in the water that comes out of the average Westside home, but that's not an argument against what I'm saying. In fact, it just makes more sense. The DWP is fucking with the health of people of color in Los Angeles in order to reduce the population and thereby have more water and more everything for whites.

Wouldn't the women in these communities go to their doctors to get tested when they stopped getting pregnant?

What doctors? The ones that aren't there or the ones they can't afford? To get tests they can't pay for? Besides, it's not like, taken in isolation, some of these women don't want birth control. Individually, they may be perfectly fine with it.

Who came up with this?

Harry Lime.

That guy? He's still wearing a windbreaker from high school. No fucking way.

Take it from me. He's a pretty twisted, racist motherfucker.

I can't say that I was any more convinced, but I couldn't argue with her. If she was a conspiracy nut, then it wouldn't matter what I said. She would have an explanation. Petunia went back to reading and sorting her papers while I puzzled on it. Whether or not I believed that some racists at the DWP were trying to lower the population of people of color in Los Angeles as a way to kill two birds with one stone—solve the water crisis and eliminate minorities—I did believe that the men chasing Petunia Biggars had killed the Nutty Professor. So, it wasn't hard to deduce that, conspiracy or not, there was something in these documents that someone—the DWP or the government—did not want to see the light of day. Did it matter what that something was? Did I have to believe in it or even understand it? I decided I didn't.

Okay, Petunia …

She held up her hand, palm facing me.

So, I've been thinking about this whole me Petunia and dog Petunia thing you've got going here.

And?

I know I said before that I didn't know how I felt about it, but now I do. It's not gonna work.

My stomach flipped.

And not just because it's confusing to have two creatures with the same name living in the same place, but because I'm not really a Petunia with my friends. I haven't been since I was a baby. I've always been Una. Sometimes Toon, sometimes Pet, but mostly Una, a silly nickname my brother gave me. So, that's how it's got to be. That dog, for saving me from the big bad clowns from the DWP, gets to be Petunia, and I get to be who I am: Una. And you, without really earning it, get to pretend we're friends. Okay?

I wasn't certain that she was finished, so I didn't say anything.

Okay?

She said, raising her voice to make her point.

Okay

I said.

Now start over.

Okay, Una, so you want to develop a movie that exposes this conspiracy—and you want my help to do that.

It was a statement. Probably should have been a question.

Where'd you get that idea?

She was irritated again.

From Dr. Holly. Who else would think you could base a movie on DWP lab reports?

Not the movie part, the *you* part. The part where we want your help. She told you that?

More or less. She knew I was Samson. Clearly, you'd told her about me. That's why she met me. That's why she gave me the key. She didn't have to spell it out. I just did the math. Una wants a movie. Movie needs a screenplay. I'm a screenwriter. On your mark, get set—

That's not the math.

She was curt.

You can't help me with the creative part, but I guess you're right that I do want something.

And what is that—saving you from the bad guys?

When I showed up at your door, with all this evidence, it wasn't because I thought you could save me. It was because I'd seen you and Shemahn at the Blacks Only meeting—

Attacked us, you mean.

That was only to keep the really angry people from beating on you.

And I suppose I should thank you for that?

Let's not get sidetracked please, but no, I didn't do it for you. I did it for the POCs who would've been beaten or killed by the cops for laying a finger on you. We don't need to go around confirming what all those racist assholes are claiming about us. Like King said, we need to be better, less violent.

Fine, no sidetracks into who saved whom. If you don't want my help developing this conspiracy into a movie, what do you want? And let me give you a heads-up. Whatever made you knock on my door better be worth completely fucking up my life.

I could see by her reaction that she doubted I would think it was.

Spit it out.

To meet Shemahn.

You gotta be kidding me! I'm not her fuckin' personal assistant. You know she has an agent and a manager for stuff like this.

They wouldn't return my call.

For good reason—you're a nobody in Hollywood.

Honestly, I didn't know anything about Shemahn or you before you showed up at the meeting, but when I did my research, I read how you saved her life and how the two of you were developing projects together. You know, I thought, this conspiracy's just what they're looking for. So, seeing as how I didn't have another option for reaching Shemahn, I decided to use you to get the project to her.

Okay, great. You decided to use me. Great, except that now we're both trapped. Stuck, might as well be chained together like Poitier and Curtis in *The Defiant Ones*. What's your next bright idea?

I guess it's out of the question that you call Shemahn for me?

I don't really see why I should help with a project I'm not attached to.

To stop a crime against humanity? Isn't that enough?

It would be if were true.

Trust me, it's true.

Okay, let's say you are telling the truth—or that I believe you are. In that case, we should be going to the police or the EPA or the United Nations if you don't trust anyone in the US government. We should be blowing whistles—not trying to make a movie out of this crime. Development could take years if it ever even happens, and a lot of innocent POCs could have their lives ruined in the meantime.

I raised my hand to stop her justifications before I was finished.

On the other hand, what you told me makes more sense as a conspiracy movie, if what we're saying seems plausible, but we don't claim is actually based on a true story.

I lowered my hand. She jumped.

Even if we blew the whistle and stopped Lime, the government would bury the evidence. The people would never know what happened to them. We need publicity. Game-changing publicity. That's where Shemahn comes in.

Hire a public relations firm then. Or if you still think your only option is to get to Shemahn, then figure out how to use me so that I don't feel used.

She needed a minute to consider this.

How can you be part of this, Samson? This is an African American project.

For Blacks Only.

Exactly.

No whites involved in any way—not even as villains?

She nodded about the villains, but then she came at me from another, practical angle.

How can we work together if we don't trust each other?

Una wasn't afraid to speak her mind, so I decided I wouldn't be either. I figured the *we* she was referring to was just as much *we* Una and Sam as *we* black and white.

You're full of it if you think trust is always about race—not with me anyway. White, black, Asian, Latino, it wouldn't have mattered who rang my doorbell. Think of all the people who didn't stop to help that guy in the Bible, a guy who was really hurt. And you weren't bleeding. You hadn't been robbed. You had an expensive bike. You were beautiful. Just because I'm not some fucking Samaritan doesn't mean I'm untrustworthy. So, before you indict me for not trusting you, check the windows in your own glass house.

She digested this.

Please don't forget that I was happy for you to wait on my porch for the police. And also remember that when you crash-landed in my bathtub, I didn't push you back out the window. Before you make this out to be black and white, you need to account for all of my behavior—and yours. You came here for help. Twice.

I stopped to give her a chance to tell me I was full of shit—it would always be black and white.

She didn't. In fact, she wasn't doing anything. She was standing across the table from me with her fingers resting lightly on the tops of two stacks of paper, leaving greasy fingerprints, her head tilted forward slightly so that I could not see her eyes or her expression. The only movement I could see was the gentle rise of her chest from her breathing.

Then, without any premeditation, I found myself apologizing.

Hey, even so, I'm sorry about not letting you in the other day. I know I made a mistake.

Thursday, 9:10 a.m.

What is a grip exactly?

We'd been standing in silence at my dining room table for more than ten minutes. I didn't see where Una was going with her question, so figuring she was just one more person satisfying her curiosity about the inside baseball of the movie business, I gave my stock answer.

Grips mainly work with the camera, putting it where the cameraman wants it, moving it when it needs to move, rigging it, dollies, insert cars, and the like. We also help the electricians, not with the lights—we don't touch those— but sometimes the lights need something in front of them or around them, they're called flags and gels, or to be protected from the rain.

Where does saving someone's life fit into that?

As the key grip, I also try to keep an eye on things, make sure it's a safe set, but frankly, safety's everyone's responsibility: the first AD, the stunt coordinator, and the producer, for starters.

If it's everyone's responsibility, how come Shemahn tells everyone it was you?

Simple. I saw something was wrong, and I pointed it out.

I don't need simple. I need complicated.

Oh. Una wasn't asking about grips; she was asking about my relationship with Shemahn. It wasn't hard to figure out why; she wanted to know if I was really standing in her way. I didn't see how the story of what happened would matter, so I told it.

We were shooting a car chase through downtown. Round Disney Hall. Near the 110. Shemahn was playing the daughter of this good-guy embezzler from the mob; she's in one car with her dad who's been shot, trying to get him to the hospital, they're being chased by this evil dude's henchmen who are trying to kill him for what he did and then kidnap Shemahn's character to sell her to sex traffickers or something. Anyway, we'd already done of bunch of Shemahn's shots on green screen, but then the director—this punk kid electronic press kit newbie—got it into his head that he couldn't have 'bogus green-screen close-ups' in his movie. So, he talks to the stunt coordinator, and they figure out some way to get some action close-ups of Shemahn driving with the evil dude stunt guys' cars swerving behind and just missing her. And then the punk talks to Shemahn and tells her it will be completely safe and that all she's got to do is drive straight ahead on a completely controlled road so nothing can happen. He convinces her it'll be fun—and she'll be able to brag on the publicity tour about how she's the real deal doing her own stunts.

So we're having our last safety meeting before belting her in, and I'm listening to the stunt coordinator explain exactly what's gonna happen and what speeds everyone's gonna be going. He's got his Hot Wheels out, and he's pushing them around a toy block diorama of the location, explaining how we'll do a half-speed rehearsal and then a full-speed one. And it all looks good, safe, and then the first AD who's a bit of a brownnose douche himself sees that Shemahn's not so confident, so he wisecracks that she'll be fine, and even if something goes wrong, it won't be any worse than a fender bender. She might get hit with an airbag. Then I see the car they're putting her into and realize it doesn't have airbags in it anymore. They stripped them all out to make room for camera equipment. I know this because I'd been rigging that same car for a different shot the day before. If her face hits anything, it'll be a camera lens—and not an airbag.

I said, 'Hold it—there aren't any airbags in this car. Plus shouldn't we do some real rehearsals with a stunt driver before you put an actor in there?'

Of course, plenty of people were pissed at me for putting the brakes on, so to speak. We might not make the day if we did a lot of unnecessary rehearsals. The AD got in my face, yelling that the people who needed to say it was safe said it was safe, that he was the one responsible for safety on the set, not me, so who was I to say no they couldn't do something that was clearly safe? So, I just said, 'Look, if you insist on putting her in that car and trying that stunt the way you're saying, then I'm walking and taking all my guys with me right now.'

That woke Shemahn up. She sat down in her cast chair behind the monitor. The director started begging her, pleading that it was safe, that I didn't know jack shit, etcetera, he'd done lots of stunts, been on *Twilight Zone,* so he would never put anyone in danger again—none of which was exactly true. Didn't matter how much he begged—she wouldn't budge. I could hear her saying that considering that they'd made up the part about there being airbags, she wouldn't guarantee she would ever do the shot. In the end, he did get her to agree not to make her mind up till she saw the rehearsal.

They did a half-speed rehearsal with the stunt girl, and it went great—not a hitch. The director puffs out his chest, and I hear him telling the producer he wants me off his set. We're all waiting for Shemahn to get in the car, but she isn't moving. 'What was that?' she says when the AD tells her the camera's ready, and he's calling for final touches. 'The rehearsal,' he says. 'But I heard you say half-speed,' she says. 'Yes, I guess it was,' he says. 'Well, I'm not going to get in that car without a full-speed rehearsal.'

The director—who was still arguing with the producer—just waves the AD to go ahead, and get it over with, which the AD does. It's all going okay at full speed until one of the stunt vehicles fishtails, comes around, and hits the back end of the car Shemahn would have been driving—and sends it spinning like a top toward an overpass.

Long story short, the stunt girl saved her own life by steering the car into a concrete bollard, thereby keeping it from pinwheeling off the overpass and dropping upside down into the live traffic on the 110. The 110 wasn't part of the set, so it wasn't closed. The car and the bollard were destroyed, but she walked away, pretty shook up and sore, and that was it.

The stunt girl told anyone who would listen that that shot was no place for an actor, but nobody was listening. And not because they were still trying to get Shemahn to do the shot. Or to get me fired. Nope. It was all about moving on, making the day after that. They dropped the shot and literally turned the camera to look the other way while the mess got cleaned up. Then they wrapped Shemahn in picture, the AD making a big show of it like they always do, gathering everybody, same old speech, it's a sad day, blah blah blah. Shemahn is finished in picture. Crew was hugging her, applauding, but she was crying, saying to me, 'What's that mean, Samson? Finished in picture? Did they cut me from the movie just because I wouldn't get in the car?' 'No,' I said, laughing and hugging her. It just means that it was your last shot. It's a good thing for you.' She looked shell-shocked as she walked away, but I was happy for her. I knew that punk director had all the coverage of her he needed anyway.

Una sneered and said

The myth of the white savior rides again.

No. Nothing like that. I was just doing my job—the same way I would for anyone. Like I would have even for that punk director or douche first AD. Actually, Shemahn saved her own life by insisting on the full-speed rehearsal. 'Course I don't think she would have been killed. Hurt maybe. Shemahn was the one who came up with that life-saving angle. No matter what I said, she had her version and wouldn't be talked out of it. Media savvy, I guess. Then after the movie wrapped, she invited me over to her house and asked if I liked being a grip. I said it wasn't the be-all end-all, but it paid the bills, and she said, 'What if *I* pay your bills so you can produce a movie with me?' The next thing you know, we started Samson Productions. That's the story.

Did she name the company that—or did you?

That was her idea. She said she didn't want to forget what I'd done for her.

Was you being the screenwriter also her idea?

As a matter of fact, she did say she wouldn't mind if I were a hyphenate.

Hyphenate?

Writer-producer. You want to be a hyphenate in Hollywood.

And you were a writer before you were a grip?

No.

But you've written screenplays?

Not exactly.

Then you studied writing in college?

I've been to screenwriting workshops, but I didn't go to college.

Una had a faraway look in her eye.

I went to college, but I never imagined I could write a movie

She said.

Maybe you're selling yourself short.

She didn't take the bait. She was too focused on finally getting to where she was going.

Did it ever occur to you that this whole Samson Productions—you as a producer, you as the hyphenate—was a put-up? That Shemahn doesn't really expect you to come up with an award-winning part for her? That she appreciates what you did, but she doesn't really believe in your creative talent? That she saw how you might have fucked up your life by bucking the system the way you did to save her, and she wanted to do right by you, not by giving you a handout directly but indirectly, not giving you the fish but the opportunity to learn to fish, and if you could fish in the end, great, but if you couldn't, so what? She'd still done right by you? Did that ever occur to you?

I could tell by the gentleness of Una's tone that she thought I would be undermined and devastated. I wasn't either. I mean, it wasn't like that had never crossed my mind.

Of course

I said

Yes, it also occurred to me that while I'm learning how to fish on her dime, maybe I'd get lucky and hook a big one.

So even though you say she doesn't owe you anything, you're okay with her paying the tab and never getting anything out of it.

She is getting something out of it. She's getting someone who believes she's got more to offer the world than mindless pop songs. And I'm the only one I know of who believes that, which is why I intend to produce a movie that will show what a talented actor she is.

And is she?

What?

A talented actor.

Does it matter?

To whom?

To you? Does she have to be talented to play Una ... what's your last name again, Una?

Biggars.

Does Shemahn have to be talented to play Una Biggars in Una's biopic?

What makes you think this is about me?

I may be a ridiculous old white guy who's losing his hair, but it seems pretty obvious what your water conspiracy movie—let's call it *Black Chinatown*—has to be about: a beautiful black activist teams up with a nerdy female scientist to expose a massive conspiracy. Nobody's gonna watch two hours of Harry Lime in his laboratory cackling over his beakers. We want hot, sexy, intrigue. That activist sounds like a perfect part for Shemahn. Close enough?

She finally laughed.

Close enough.

She looked down at her piles of paper and then back at me.

Okay.

Okay what?

Okay, you can write the screenplay.

We

I said. Part of me, the unchained part, felt like telling her: fuck off, I know when I'm not wanted. But I didn't. I continued.

We, we can write it. I'm not doing this by myself. We either collaborate—100 percent, fifty-fifty, partners with shared credit, shared upfront fees, shared back end, everything equal as writers, you wearing this as much as me—or we're back to square one. No way out and running out of food.

She didn't seem happy about the idea of a partnership with me. I think she had in mind her own trial by fire that would leave me scorched. She picked up a piece of paper from one pile, looked at it, moved it to another pile, and then repeated the action. She could do that all day as far as I was concerned. It didn't change anything. It might only be a cute metaphorical memory one day, but for the foreseeable future, Una and I were chained together.

I'm an activist—not a screenwriter. And besides, this is evidence, not a story.

So what? I bet you're more creative than you think.

I don't need any bullshit affirmative action, Samson. I got into college on my own merit.

This isn't affirmative action. What Shemahn did for me, as you so kindly pointed out, is affirmative action. This is just Hollywood.

You've at least been to workshops. You know the rules. Isn't there some hero's journey or something?

Sure, I know my Joseph Campbell. And I've read *Screenwriting for Dummies*. What I also know from personal experience is that if we're not partners on this, this story will never be written, the movie will never be produced, and your conspiracy will never be exposed.

She drummed her knuckles on the table and sighed.

Okay then

She opened her arms like she was going to hug me. I didn't jump into them.

Welcome to my twisted conspiratorial world, Samson.

I got my laptop and sat down on the couch.

Okay—*Black Chinatown*—it doesn't have to be the final name, but we need something to start with.

Hold on a minute. You need to read all this.

Have you read it?

Many times.

Well, that's good enough. Besides, I'm pretty sure the moviegoer will never know exactly what those say. I mean, who can remember what *Chinatown* was actually about, except water, I mean? And even if we decide to include an insert of the lab reports, it will be late in the story when the numbers won't matter as much as the conspiracy itself.

But we have to get the truth out. This is actually happening. This isn't some made-up bullshit. They're fucking with our lives.

You think that *Chinatown* wasn't about something that actually happened? The way I see it, we've got the perfect one-two punch if we can get this conspiracy right. You're right. You need publicity more than a recitation of the facts. If the conspiracy is scary enough, then Shemahn brings the story to everyone's attention and creates an Academy Award buzz, and then right when she's accepting the best actress Oscar from Tom Hanks instead of thanking the director and her agent and her makeup artist, she brings up her producer, Una Biggars, and reveals that this whole thing really happened and that there's front-page story tomorrow in the *LA Times* with the sordid truth and outing Dr. Harry Lime.

Maybe

She didn't seem entirely convinced.

Look, we can figure out how much factual reality we want in as we go along, but first, we have to build our tough but beloved main character. Our Erin Brockovich. We need to start with the Hollywood version of Petunia Biggars, our heroine, *you*.

Una stared off into space. I had no idea what she was thinking.

Mind if I make some coffee?

She headed toward the kitchen.

Good idea. Look in the canister on the counter.

I watched the cursor pulse on my empty screen.

C'mon Samson, I thought, fade in, fade in. You can write it. Fade in. Then I remembered something else.

Oh, and Una?

Yes?

She appeared in the kitchen door holding the empty coffeepot.

It would be a good idea if we could come up with a young transgender character who's a songwriter transitioning from male to female.

Why?

Short answer: office politics, but trust me, it would eliminate some hoops if we could.

Okay then.

She headed back into the kitchen. A few moments later, she reappeared. The glass coffeepot was halfway full of water.

What if the transgender kid works at the DWP? He's a lab tech or junior scientist or—

I jumped in.

Who's actually a songwriter trying to get his music career going, but he's kind of a pariah there, harassed. His boss bullies him.

And his boss is Harry Lime. And the kid stumbles on the conspiracy and gets the evidence to Shemahn.

Her turn. My turn. Just like that, we were riffing off each other. It was fun. We were having fun. Both of us doing something we weren't supposed to be able to do. Then I remembered something.

What about Dr. Martins? Take her out?

Una's face fell like it was the end of the carnival ride. She'd forgotten about Dr. Martins.

I had no intention of giving up on our partnership.

How about if the transgender kid is her son? Dr. Martins is killed right in the beginning, after she goes to a Blacks Only meeting to try to give the lab reports to the beautiful young activist. Her son doesn't believe she's committed suicide like the police say. He teams up with the black activist.

Who's also an aspiring singer.

She was excited again.

And he writes her a song.

Samson, old boy, I thought, maybe what you've been missing all along was a partner. Maybe now your agony is *finito*.

Thursday, A Couple Hours Later

I was surprised how right I was when I told Una the story wouldn't get written without her. We decided to skip the treatment and go right to a full script. There wasn't any point or time to waste. Working together, we jammed through a third of the screenplay, scene after scene flowing out of our collaboration; there was no denying the synergy.

Not that I'm a jazz aficionado, but it felt like that to me: the two of us going back and forth, taking turns, playing one moment and then another, improvising dialogue, feeding off each other. The inspiration was flowing and flowing only because we were partners. I had heard in my classes how much fun other writers had when things were on a roll, but I had never known that high. It was part of the reason that, deep down, I didn't think I was a writer. With Una, the scenes practically wrote themselves—faster than I could type them sometimes—piling up like there was no tomorrow. Except, of course, I knew there had to be a tomorrow because there was no way we had the stamina to write a 120-page screenplay in one nonstop session. We had to hold onto enough of the flow to have it on the second and the third and the fourth day.

We need a break

I said

Get out of our heads a little, maybe get some exercise, refill the tank.

Sure.

Una laughed and smiled her crooked, mocking smile.

Shall we go for bike ride and let those DWP clowns chase us? You can ride on my handlebars.

My phone rang before I could think of a good wisecrack. It was my Ex. She wanted to know if I'd heard anything about the charges against Atticus or the date of his arraignment.

We know what they'll be. Attempted murder. That's the charge.

Maybe the prosecutor won't see it that way.

I doubt it, but we'll know soon enough.

We need to get him a lawyer.

Be a good idea.

Maybe one of your crew friends, Angel or Alex, knows one. Maybe Alex's manager. What's his name?

Milt Milton. I don't know. He's a pretty big deal.

Well, maybe Alex would ask him for us.

Maybe.

We need the best, Samson. Atticus is not cut out for prison.

I knew she was about to lose it.

Who is? But we have to face reality. There might not be a lot we can do to change his fate. And besides …

Besides what?

It may not be the best thing for Atticus, but it might be the best thing for the rest of us to lock him up for awhile. I haven't even begun to process his trying to kill me.

She didn't respond.

I'll call you after I talk to Angel and Alex.

Okay, well, I have the cash for his guys—if you want to come and get it.

Hang onto it for a bit, if you don't mind. That can wait till things settle down.

My Ex

I explained to Una as I dialed Angel.

He picked up on the second ring.

You'll love this one!

There was no shoe leather with Angel. We'd known each other too long—shared too many long nights on the set— to bother with small talk. He was bursting to tell me, so I let him.

We're on the Fox lot, rigging the process trailer to kill time. We're back on first unit. Insurance day. Last two days of the picture. All we got left is Jesse's driving to work with his love interest, but he's at the plastic surgeon. Numbnuts tore a hole in his nose trying to pop a zit, and now he won't let the girl see him because he still hasn't fucked her. So, the entire company's sitting around until the production manager has covered his ass with the insurance company.

What a fuckin' idiot!

It is what it is. I have to say she *is* hot. Hey, I'm sorry to hear things went tits up with Shemahn.

It shouldn't have, but Angel took me completely by surprise. I mean, I've had more than thirty years of hearing stories of how people in Hollywood turned on each other or screwed each other or flat-out betrayed their partners. I should have been on the lookout. Even before the conversation with

Ja'K about my pages going to him first, I knew that he was a snake in the grass, but I guess I was just so high from finally busting through my nonwriter's block that I wasn't watching my blindside.

With anyone else I would have pretended, but I said

What are you talking about?

Oh, shit. Sorry. They said it was mutual.

What was mutual?

Creative differences, I don't remember exactly.

Angel was backtracking like he couldn't believe how badly he'd stepped in it.

C'mon, Angel. Cut the crap. Give it to me without any soft serve.

Okay.

He took a deep breath.

There was an interview with her and her director in *Variety* about her next picture. Samson Productions isn't mentioned, so the reporter asks what's happened with you and Sam Agonistes. Her agent says there were creative differences, and you all have agreed to pursue separate projects for the time being, but you're still friends, and they have the utmost respect for your talent, you know, the same old BS.

Who's the director?

Some unknown, foreign-sounding, what's-his-name

He called out to one of his guys

What's the name of that director for the Shemahn picture?

Then, just like that, we said the name simultaneously:

Ja'K.

Yeah, that's it. You know him?

A week ago, he was her assistant. Did they say what the picture was?

Sure. Something to do with minority rights, LGBTQ, I think.

No Blacks Only?

To be honest, pal. I don't remember. You want me to ask the guys?

Don't bother.

Sorry to be the bearer of bad news.

Don't be. If there's anywhere in America where your story changes while you're telling it, it's Hollywood. Don't worry about me. I'll survive. As things stand in my life, that's not even the worst of it. Atticus was arrested last night.

Oh, shit. What for?

He hasn't been charged yet, but one thing's for sure: it'll involve assault with a handgun.

Guns? I wouldn't have expected that from your kid.

It is what it is.

There was a moment of silence as we both reflected on this epitaph of parenting.

Anyhow, if you happen to know any lawyers, I'd appreciate a referral.

I don't know one personally, but let me ask around.

Needs to be a good one.

I get it. Maybe I'll ask Jesse. Actors like him are always in trouble.

Great idea.

From the bathroom, Una called out

What will you survive?

I didn't answer. I was surfing the web for Shemahn news. Not that I planned on keeping anything from Una, but I had hoped to catch my breath before unloading my troubles. Una came down the hallway with Petunia trailing after her. When she stopped, the cone hit the back of her knees, but she didn't jump.

Did I hear you say something like 'no Blacks Only'?

She made air quotes.

I hope you realize that, taken out of context, that doesn't sound good.

It seemed like she was about to get upset.

It was a question

I said

But look at this, and you'll understand.

I'd clicked on a YouTube of the press conference. Shemahn and Ja'K were sitting at a table with an obese guy who was identified as Milt Milton, my director friend Alex's new manager, the one with the missing Big Gulp, the one my Ex wanted me to ask about a lawyer for Atticus. Small world— but not in the good way. Milton managed all the top talent, so it was natural that he'd be working with Shemahn. It just surprised me that she hadn't mentioned him before.

Milton was doing all the talking. He confirmed the details. Samson Productions was out. Ja'K would direct. Shemahn would play the founder of a political movement who finds inspiration to expose a secret government conspiracy to suppress minorities after the murder of her best friend, a trans kid. That was it—except that Shemahn refused to answer any questions.

What's that fat guy have against you?

Una asked.

Milt Milton? Beats me. I've never met the guy, but he's one of the most powerful people in Hollywood. And if he says someone's having creative differences, that's what the town believes. Bottom line, he's telling the world, whatever it is Shemahn's doing next, it's not what you and I are working on.

So, we're out?

That's the story they'd like us to believe anyway.

I don't understand.

Did you see the expression on Shemahn's face when they tried to ask her questions about Samson Productions? That's the same expression she had when they tried to get her in the car after the half-spced rehearsal. She's biding her time. Saving herself, so to speak. She's not getting in whatever car Milt Milton's driving without a full-speed rehearsal. My guess is that, even though they've announced the project, they don't have a script.

Still, it sounds pretty close to what we're doing.

Yes.

How do you know they don't have a script?

Because that's the idea Ja'K pitched to me two days ago. More or less. I mean there were a lot of ideas batted around. We didn't settle on anything—except that I was supposed to write up what we talked about.

Okay, so how do you know they don't have another writer working already? What if that kid drove straight from your house to Aaron Sorkin's or Callie Khouri's. Writers like that could already be done as far as you know.

That's not likely ... if I know anything about Hollywood. It would take weeks to cut a deal, let alone settle on a treatment.

I took a beat.

Listen, this kid started as her assistant a month ago. He was a little shit, but it was clear he was political. He got her ear and wangled his way into being a producer. That's what he was when he showed up here to talk to me and insert the trans kid story line. Then he calls me to inform me that all my contact with Shemahn has to go through him. Classic Hollywood gatekeeper move. Then they make an announcement that they have a project that's the story line they both want: trans issues plus oppressed minorities. And watch out—he's now the director. So, then, what's his next move? Write the script that they pitched, right? Except it won't go like that. First of all, because he's not a writer, and second of all, he doesn't want a Blacks Only story. He wants a story that's about him, one that he can use to leapfrog all of us—even Shemahn. He's using her too, which is why we have to finish our script as soon as possible.

So what if he's not a writer

She said

We're not writers either. I don't know if we're anything but captives of the deep state at this point. Don't take this wrong, Samson, but I'm worried that I'm wasting my time here. I need to be doing whatever I can to contact Shemahn directly.

I can see how you might think that, but say you show Shemahn the evidence and even convince her to make a movie out of it, you'll still end up outside her door with someone like me or Ja'K or Milt Milton. That's just how it works. Celebrities may not like their gatekeepers, but they need them.

But you're not even outside her door anymore, are you? You're just making the case that I should be working with one of those other guys: Ja'K or the fat one.

No, actually I'm not. Forget Ja'K. He's nothing. Milton's the one to worry about, and I wouldn't put my fate in Milt Milton's hands if I were you. Besides if we can get around them, we'll be back in business. And, believe me, I know how to get around gatekeepers. We'll finish our script before they do. And when we do, Shemahn will be in our parade instead of theirs. So, don't give up on us yet. We're on a roll.

C'mon, Samson. We have to stop kidding ourselves. We have no idea what we're doing. It's kind of pathetic to think we can change the world from a smelly dump in Mar Vista. We need to find a real writer.

Maybe we already have. Maybe it's us. Maybe we're real writers in spite of ourselves. I mean, it's going great, and we're having fun, aren't we? Admit it—you're having fun.

Yes. I'll admit it, but having fun isn't the same thing as good writing.

Why not?

I don't think real writers have fun. They're head cases.

I hope you're wrong about that, but in any case, I think there's another thing to consider. What if you were right before when you said this whole Samson Productions was Shemahn's idea of affirmative action? Well, if that's true, then she isn't going to green-light just anybody's script. It doesn't matter what Ja'K comes up with. She doesn't owe him her life. So, she's waiting for mine. That's what the look on her face says. And mine—ours—is pretty damn far along and pretty damn good, if I don't say so myself.

Una didn't respond. She was lost in thought until an aggressive push from Petunia buckled her knees. She regained her balance and patted the cone absentmindedly.

Is Atticus your son?

I couldn't read her expression.

Yes.

And you think he's going to be charged with attempted murder because he tried to kill you?

I'm not the only one he took a shot at, but yes. I'd rather not talk about that if you don't mind.

Sure. I guess.

Short break and then back at it?

Sure

She said, but I heard hesitation.

Something else bothering you?

Yes, actually.

She looked up at me.

Shemahn's announcing her project like that could've been a mistake.

Why? Isn't that kind of what we're going for? Publicity.

Sure, but you don't rub what you're doing in the government's face, do you? It's okay to tease a conspiracy—but don't have it be a secret government one.

Why not?

I told you these people are doing everything they can to keep minorities from changing this country to a place where white people don't have all the privilege. They're spying on us, sowing dissent in our movements, and spreading rumors. They're doing *whatever* it takes, and when the powers that be think they can't silence you in any other way, they kill you.

You think they'll try to silence Shemahn?

Absolutely. They don't just come after activists like me.

But if that's basically the same movie we've been writing, how did you think we would get away with making it without putting Shemahn's life at risk?

All our lives—even yours. Sometimes they like race-betrayers even less.

Okay, all our lives. Don't tell me this is only just now occurring to you?

It's not.

So how were you planning to keep us all from falling out of a window or being hit by a bus?

I got the idea from you actually: cinematic immunity.

I cracked up. She was serious.

Are you kidding? Cinematic immunity is just a dumb thing that movie people say to each other when they've screwed up and waltzed in someplace they don't belong, like a riot or a prison yard full of twenty-five-to-lifers who haven't had lunch.

Or a Blacks Only meeting?

Sure.

But it worked, didn't it? You're here. You made it out alive.

Telling a bunch of angry black people you're with the movie might keep you from getting beat up, but it isn't going to keep the government from putting you six feet under.

I disagree. I believe it's the only safe way to get this story told.

You were asking about trust before. Well, trust me, cinematic immunity is a joke. It's not real. It's the emperor's new clothes.

White supremacy is a joke too, but look what that's done for you folks.

I shook my head. She nodded hers.

Think about it, Samson. The people who are in the most danger in this society are the ones we've never heard of till after they're dead.

But that's not Shemahn.

It's relative, Samson. At this moment, to the deep state, she is a nobody. They'll be able to make up whatever story they want about her—same as they would about me. America's not going to think it's strange if her plane goes down or she ODs. Think of Buddy Holly or Jimi Hendrix or Tupac. Shemahn doesn't get a pass just because she's got a fan club. She has to use her fame. Make it work for her, make it serve her mission of staying alive. Like Beyoncé. She speaks the truth, but because she's so famous, her life and politics are so public, they can't assassinate her. Shemahn doesn't have that luxury yet. That's what I mean by she might have made a mistake. We should have had time to build up her immunity before she exposed herself. As it is now, they could kill her and get away with it. Call it whatever you want, but what I'm talking about is real and will work. And I'm going to call it cinematic immunity.

So, you had a plan for how to immunize her?

Absolutely, once we have Shemahn on board, we'll start to work on everyone's immunity, slowly, without calling attention to ourselves. Shemahn will have to fly under the government radar until the movie is in the can ... is that right, in the can?

In the can, sure.

The film is in the can is kind of like a letter with the incriminating evidence left with your lawyer; then she can start predicting and publicizing the likely government attempt to silence her. She'll do it at her concerts, on the web, and on talk shows. Once she has a campaign like that attached to a full-on truth-telling, no way they can kill her. She'll be safe. We all will be.

In his attempt to ace me out, Milt Milton has put a target on her back—and she doesn't even know it.

Una nodded.

I know you said you were just doing your job before when you kept her from getting into that car, and I get why you think you didn't actually save her life, that she wasn't really in that much danger. Well, you have to believe me.

Shemahn is going to be killed, unless we—you and I—figure out how to save her.

How? We're in solitary confinement, remember?

Una nodded.

To start with, we need someone on the outside to help us—someone who cares as much about Shemahn as we do.

We looked at each other and said simultaneously

Ja'K!

Hold on, does a user really care about the person they're using?

Una said.

She's his meal ticket. He has to help us. He won't have a choice. I'll convince him.

I said that like I'd solved all our problems. Then, in the next moment, I recognized that it was a brand-new impossibility now that I was off the picture.

How the fuck do we get that little shit to come to us?

Then my doorbell rang.

Thursday, Ten Seconds Later

Speak of the devil

I said as I swung open the door.

Una and Petunia were hiding behind my transformed P. Biggars's bike/found-art-installation and the Santa Anas were rattling my windows. But, given the way the world worked, who else could it be but Ja'K? Which it was. The relief and hope I felt almost overwhelmed me. I had never been happier to see someone I thought so little of, but it wasn't Ja'K who responded.

I didn't hear my name, did you, my boy?

Whoever it was, I didn't know his voice—but he knew me.

Come out on the porch and have a chat, Samson. It's such a nice morning.

I heard the groaning protest of my bungalow's framing under extreme duress as I closed the door and stepped past Ja'K out onto my porch just as Milton J. Milton, my only recently revealed nemesis, finished settling himself on my porch swing, testing the weight-bearing limits of both the swing and the structural beam it was bolted into.

You know me, right?

He half smiled and half sucked air into his mouth as if he had something stuck in his teeth.

Not really

I said, pretending I could keep the upper hand with such a heavy hitter.

He looked like a cross between that incredibly fat crocodile Tick Tock that chases Captain Hook through the Disney movie and Mickey Rourke in *Angel Heart*. His head was too small and kind of square for the average crocodile, and he was wearing a custom-tailored suit that hid his scales, but I recognized a reptile when I saw one.

Really? That's disappointing.

He crocodile smiled. Juvenile Hollywood games like that didn't dent his ego.

But I suppose that explains our initial miscommunication so many months ago. I'm Milton J. Milton. I'm—

That your real name?

I interrupted to keep him off balance, but it didn't work. He knew all the tricks.

At the moment. Is Samson Agonistes yours?

He returned fire.

Once upon a time. On set.

So, not happily ever after?

No.

What's the matter with Tinseltown these days, Samson? Remember the good old days when being born Hirsz Wonskolaser or Margarita Cansino wasn't as important as turning into a real American. Almost makes you lose faith in the dream factory.

He was beckoning to Ja'K as he spoke.

Come, my boy, sit.

With his spade-shaped paw, he patted the tiny square of the swing that wasn't overrun by his obese-ness.

I shivered. Is he kidding? Putting more stress on that beam?

Ja'K brushed past me and nestled himself in next to Milt.

The house protested more emphatically. I heard a sharp crack in the beam above their heads. I looked up, expecting the worst, but there was nothing visibly scary. The bolts somehow seemed to be holding. Then the chain links started popping at odd intervals—like the last kernels of the popcorn before you pull the pot from the flame. Milt was using the fat, big toes of his triangular crocodile feet to push the swing. I had to drop the smart-ass and warn them before someone got hurt.

I don't know …

I pointed toward the ceiling. It was his turn to interrupt.

What Milt Milton is doing sitting on your porch with the hot new directorial talent Ja'K? I can imagine, after the press conference we gave ending your partnership with my client, that you might be thinking this was your lucky day. That you still had a future.

I didn't say what I was thinking.

Tap, tap, squeak, squeak, pop, pop, pop, pop, pop. The sides of the house were lifting off the foundation with every pendulum back and forth. Like the posts of a swing set that hasn't been set in concrete lifting out of the ground as your kid swings higher and higher, right before the whole thing tips over and kills someone.

Milt Milton waved the hand that he had rested on Ja'K's shoulder to dismiss his own idea.

No, I'm sorry. This is not your lucky day, Samson. Your future came and went some time ago. And I must confess that what concerns me now is the fact that if you were too stupid to recognize your lucky day, does that mean you're also too stupid to recognize the dead-end street you've gone down.

My Ex never understood why I couldn't ask for directions.

Milt raised an eyebrow.

In all honesty, do you not remember talking to my assistant at the *Crashing Bores* premiere? Do you not remember that he asked you to come to the VIP room so that we could discuss a very lucrative multipicture deal?

I shook my head, even as I was mentally kicking myself, not for blowing him off since I actually had no memory of talking to his assistant, but for allowing him to know I blew him off. You didn't want Milt Milton pissed at you.

It was pretty noisy, as I recall, and I was drunk. Sorry.

It was a lame excuse.

What deal were you offering?

What does it matter? It's too late for deals.

Just curious.

Suffice it to say, I would have offered you and Shemahn everything everyone in this town wants: money, fame, artistic credibility.

And I turned that down? Doesn't sound like me. I think maybe you got the wrong guy.

Your response was something along the lines of two's company, three's a crowd.

Yeah, like I said, Milt, I think your assistant got me confused with a real dipshit. I've been around long enough to know when Milt Milton offers you something, it's a deal you can't refuse.

Milt stopped sucking his teeth and studied me from under heavy lids. I didn't look away. The truth was I'd gotten so full of myself after becoming Shemahn's partner that I'd broken the cardinal rule of the movie business: never disrespect a stranger. Clearly, I'd fucked up big-time at the premiere after-party, but I didn't have to admit that. And maybe Milt would let my little lie save face for him. Or maybe he wouldn't.

That makes me sound like I'm a gangster, like I don't want what's best for everyone.

I shrugged.

So, is that why you're sitting on my porch? To offer me the best version of my non-existent future.

Well

He said

I think you can appreciate that when I say the 'best for everyone,' I don't mean the best is the same for all people. Take your ex-partner Shemahn, for example. What's best for her is to focus her creative talents—

On the script you and your hot young protégé, Ja'K, bring her.

I finished his sentence as if I could prove something by it. Milton sneered and shook his head.

On her music. She'll never be a leading lady in Hollywood. Acting is her dead-end street.

That surprised me; all of sudden dead-end streets were popping up all around me.

You think writing bubblegum pop songs that end up in cosmetic commercials is better for Shemahn than acting? Than taking charge of her creative future and producing?

We all have to accept our limits in life, Samson. Shemahn will see that. I mean, she really doesn't want to 'produce' as you and I understand that concept. Frankly, it's beyond her. As for the acting? Why would she want to damage her brand that way? We just need to manage her perspective enough to show her what's best for her.

What does that mean exactly?

I assume you caught our press conference. Confidentially, I will share with you that in spite of how it might have seemed, I'm killing that project this very afternoon. I have another picture for Shemahn. She'll have a small part, nothing too taxing. She'll play a singer. And not some self-important Blacks Only activist. Americans want movies about the happiness of all—not the problems of a few. It's too disorienting.

I glanced at Ja'K. He was staring at his hands in his lap, riding the Milt Milton ride.

So, the movie you will let her make is about a transgender kid who writes pop songs? The one Ja'K pitched me earlier this week? The one where Shemahn only has a cameo?

That would be the best thing for her. I certainly couldn't allow a major talent like Shemahn to suffer from any guilt by association.

Association with whom?

The wrong kind of people. Pessimistic, unpatriotic people. Malcontents. Like that Petunia Biggars woman. We don't need movies about her and her supposed struggle. What good does it do America? It won't change anything. All Blacks Only does is create bad feelings. Frankly, Samson, I'm surprised that you wouldn't agree with me about this. We all know we live in the greatest country in the history of mankind—as long as we keep it that way.

And what happens if she won't go along?

But she will. Ja'K will make sure of that.

Ja'K didn't chime in to confirm that, but he didn't need to.

Ja'K? Really? He can't make her do anything.

I wouldn't underestimate him if I were you, Samson. He's been preparing for a long time for just this mission.

I thought he just wanted to be rich and famous like every other asshole in Hollywood. What's your deal, Ja'K? You a mole with a top-secret mission?

I asked him directly even though I didn't expect him to answer. Milt put his hand in Ja'K's back and firmly pushed him off the swing.

Help me up, my boy.

It took all of Ja'K's strength, but after several tries, he did manage to use the swing's momentum to get Milt up on his feet. I could have helped, but why would I want to help a crocodile? Besides, I didn't want to be anywhere near him if he brought the porch ceiling down, which he did. Everything—beams, chains, swing—crashed onto the porch floor the instant Milt Milton and his protégé were out from under them. Milton stood next to me, smoothed his suit, and surveyed the damage.

You need to fix this dump up, Samson. Don't want your neighbors complaining about you. Calling in the authorities. Getting your home condemned. That won't help your case against the insurance company.

He gestured toward the street.

Wait for me in the car please, my boy.

Having not said a word to me, Ja'K did as he was told.

Nice talking to you too, Ja'K.

I felt full of myself until I saw the car he got into: a Maserati. It was the same color as the one I'd seen in Chinatown right before I found the Nutty Professor squashed to death.

Milt watched me put the pieces together and smiled his crocodile smile. He pulled an engraved silver Big Gulp-sized cup out of a tote bag and put the straw in his mouth.

That boy's like a son to me

Milt said as he slurped

I found him in a film production class at CSUN. Completely lost. Not a clue. He wanted to be in the film business, but he didn't want to get his hands dirty. I pulled him right out of there, trained him, and sent him out into the world. His shining moment was when I introduced him to Shemahn at a Grammy after-party. What a triumph! It was love at first sight. So to speak.

Another slurp.

Ja'K's achieved so much in such a short time, but I fear he's peaked. And that's quite a disappointment to me. It's a powerful feeling helping young people find their way, parenting if you will. You put your all into making a man …

Slurp.

Ah … what can you do? As the poet said, when the matter is ready, the form will come.

The bottom of the cup was resting on his chest, and he was staring at me with the wide, dead eyes of a sociopath.

But what am I telling you this for? You have your own parental disappointments. Your own son is quite lost, is he not?

He was showing me all his teeth.

I know where he is

I said, pitting my Samson against his beast.

Quibble over semantics all day long. Safe to say he's lost to you.

He snapped his massive jaws.

As Jesus said, if you love something, set it free

I said, verbally slipping around behind him. He writhed. I held on for dear life.

He also said that the greatest thing you'll ever learn is to love and be loved in return. I feel very lucky that all my Hollywood *sons* still love me. It must be hard not to have Atticus's love.

Just like that he wriggled away.

I'm thinking, Samson, that prison will be very hard on your boy. I'm sorry I can't recommend a good lawyer for you. I know it would break my heart for my son to spend one minute behind bars. No matter what he did. Even if he had tried to kill me.

I never had a chance.

Turn over any rock is right, Una, I thought, find yourself an evil reptile. Milt Milton had been listening in on my conversations, and now he's using them to take a bite out of me, but I made sure he didn't like the way I tasted.

Probably need a good lawyer yourself. After what you were up to in Chinatown the other night.

He spat me out, waved me off, and patted my dunlap.

Please tell me you have a good doctor, Samson. You have to take care of yourself, you know, lose that belly fat. I've found that we men of a certain background, as we get older, we need to be very mindful of our health. There's so much out there conspiring to do us in. Me, I'm under strict orders from my doctor to maintain constant hydration. Otherwise, my skin will dry up and flake off like a snake's. Can you imagine what I would look like constantly shedding? Of course, it's not like a little freshening up would kill me.

One China ring a bell?

Ah. Yes. That's a special place, but I hear the food is mediocre. I'm sure I wasn't anywhere near anything I shouldn't be if that's what you're implying, Samson. Ja'K will swear to that.

Him?

Certainly. He's very good at staying on message.

I bobbed my head toward the DWP Upgrades who were staring at us like shelter dogs in an ASPCA commercial.

How do those clowns fit into your circus?

The way all clowns do. The same way you will if you're smart.

And if I'm not?

He crocodiled me and slurped.

Sometimes it's hard to see that the end of the line is the happiest, safest place on earth for a man.

And you stopped by to help me see that?

Open your eyes to your best future.

And Shemahn? What's her best future?

Getting everything she deserves.

Courtesy of Milton J. Milton?

Well naturally.

He laughed and poked me with his spade-shaped mitt.

Maybe I was wrong about you, Samson. Maybe there is a better deal out there for you.

Forget it. I'm the one who's really lost. Not my son. But tell me, what happens if Shemahn doesn't go along and doesn't do what Milton J. Milton tells her?

He waddled down my steps.

Like I said, she'll get what she deserves.

He did not turn around. He dismissed me with a pudgy wave.

Be careful, Samson. Sometimes when a man brings his life down around his ears, it's the people he loves who get hurt the most.

Thursday, Moments Later

Forget Ja'K! That kid is the real *Manchurian Candidate*

I said.

Una was sitting on floor beside the front door with Petunia's conehead in her lap. She seemed shell-shocked.

I tried to get through the wipeout by focusing her on practicalities.

Can we stick to plan A, finish the script, and sneak it past Milton and Ja'K to Shemahn?

She came back slowly.

How long will that take?

A week, ten days, if we're being realistic. How long do we have?

Not that long. This is Thursday.

She did the math in her head as she absentmindedly stroked Petunia's ears.

I can't imagine any of us making it through the weekend now that that Milton guy has his claws in Shemahn.

What do you mean any of us? Shemahn's gotta be safe now.

I doubt it actually. Milton said he was killing the Blacks Only project, right? If she agrees, great, she'll have bought herself a little time. But even if she does let Milton manage her to the sidelines, they won't trust her to stay there.

Why not?

Because she's smart and she's already strayed once. They won't want to take a chance on her figuring out how to stray again. And they won't have to. Milton'll manage her into obscurity and then she'll disappear for real—drown drunk in a bathtub, fall down some stairs and break her neck, capsize trying to save the whales— trust me, I know how they work, she's a goner too ... unless ...

The three of us skip town, go on the lam, seek asylum in Russia

I filled in the obvious.

No

Una said and almost immediately, there was glint in her eye.

Not this again, I thought.

Hold on

She said, reading my mind.

Hear me out. What if we got Shemahn to make her publicity tour now? What if we get so far out in front of the story and make such a loud noise that the government's hands are tied. And Milton wouldn't be able to get to her either. She would be protected by her fame, by her—

Cinematic immunity

I finished.

We all would

She added.

And how would we tie the government's hands? I make my living from make believe, helping actors dodge imaginary bullets not real ones. For this, we need a real bulletproof vest, not an Emperor's.

But isn't the whole point of cinematic immunity that it's so fake it's real?

That's an untested theory.

That's about to be tested.

I didn't know what to say, so I put on my laser hair helmet and sat down on the couch.

You have any better ideas?

Una asked—even though we both knew I didn't.

Okay then. How do we get publicity? As soon as possible. Today even.

But not just today, we'll need a campaign. We'll have to keep the eyeballs once we have them.

Sure. But how?

Obviously Shemahn's the main attraction. She'll be front and center.

Main attraction. Sounds like you're imagining a circus.

Then it hit me what I was imagining.

Not exactly.

Okay?

She said

Let's hear what exactly.

And just like that we were creative partners again, bouncing ideas back and forth until we had plan.

Step one was getting someone to come to us in Mar Vista. That wasn't just because what we came up with was way too complicated to explain over the phone, particularly when the forces of evil were eavesdropping, but because we both figured that convincing this someone that we weren't conspiracy nuts would be way easier once they saw the picture's worth a thousand words of our DWP siege.

'Course finding that someone willing to subject themselves to LA traffic for no reason was easier said than done. Who was that someone? Calls coming in to me, like the ones from my Ex, were good for keeping up the cover that I was alone, holed up in my house writing. But sitting there waiting for the phone to ring wasn't in the cards. My earlier call out to Angel could have served a dual purpose, but calling him again to ask them to swing by was out of the question. The same was true with one of Una's friends or her boyfriend. That left us with only one lifeline: Petunia.

When I called the clinic, the receptionist couldn't get Hildy on the line.

He knows he's supposed to talk to Trudy

Hildy shouted from across the clinic. I could hear that she was mad.

You're supposed to talk to Trudy.

The receptionist wasn't pleased that I'd made her boss mad at her.

I'll have her call you when she's back from her break.

Sorry ... it's just that Petunia—

She hung up before I finished.

I called Hildy's cell phone over and over until she answered.

What the fuck, Dad? What about talking to my vet tech don't you understand?

This is serious. I need your help.

With what? Not Peck.

She didn't wait to hear my answer.

I know you want things to be different for him, but sooner or later, you're going to have to accept him for who he is— and then get on with your life.

Actually, it's not Atticus. It's Petunia.

That shut her up.

What's going on? She rip out her stitches again?

She won't eat or drink anything.

Is that all?

She's not acting like herself.

You haven't had her long enough to know how she acts.

Okay, well, she's not acting the same then. Yesterday she was up and about, barking her head off, and today, I can't get her to lift her head up. Her eyes are rolled back in her head.

Get her over here as soon as you can.

It hadn't occurred to us that it was obviously more efficient to bring the patient to the vet than vice versa. I said the first thing that came to mind:

I'm afraid to move her.

Why?

Well …

I stalled then lied.

She bit me.

What were you doing?

I figured she needed to go outside to pee, and I was kind of reaching under her to, you know, pick her up and—

Do you need stitches?

Oh no, it's not serious. I stopped the bleeding.

You'll need a tetanus shot.

Sure, later, after we get Petunia sorted out.

Hildy didn't say anything while she diagnosed the problem remotely.

She must be in a lot of pain

She said at last.

Definitely. How soon can you get here?

I have back-to-back patients all day.

What about lunch? Even martyrs have to eat.

Actually, I've got my only break now.

Now would be great.

The Rest of That Day through to the Last

Una and I had the Shemahn rescue and aftermath pretty well scripted—a plot we thought would work anyway—and we already had it in motion when Hildy showed up. She used her key to open the door as I was coming up from under the house and Una was dragging the last of my duffels from the bedroom toward the kitchen. Clearly, something unusual was going on.

Hildy stood on the threshold with her veterinarian bag and looked puzzled. Petunia almost blew the whole thing sky high by getting up off the bed and limping forward with her tail wagging.

This is a matter of life or death?

Hildy pointed her bag at Petunia. She was mad and heading toward madder.

I almost killed myself getting here, frantic that I'd risked this dog's life by entrusting her to you.

Petunia was ramming Hildy with her cone, but Hildy would not be put off. Una kept doing what she was doing. With my feet still in the hole I'd made in the floor, I waved my arms and tried to get my daughter to calm down.

Shut the door

I mouthed at her

Please shut the door.

She slammed it so hard the house shook.

Thank you.

I hoisted myself out of the crawl space and went to where she stood. She crossed her arms over her chest and glared at me.

I know this looks bad, but if you can please give me a moment to explain—

I knew you were lying

Hildy interrupted

I knew it, and I still came here.

She finally reached down to pet Petunia who had not stopped bumping her cone affectionately into her thigh.

Why didn't you just tell me you wanted to show off your new girlfriend?

Una popped her head out the bedroom to correct this misapprehension.

Oh, no, sister. Your white father is not my boyfriend.

Right exactly

I echoed

That's Una. She's from Blacks Only. We're working on a project together for Shemahn. And it's gotten really complicated—too complicated to explain over the phone—and kind of dangerous, and we really need your help.

Christ, Dad. I can't believe what an asshole you are sometimes. Are you ever going to give it a rest?

I can't, honey. Not while I have something to offer. But it's not just me this time. There's Una. We're partners. Listen to what she has to say and what we're asking you to do. It's not that hard, and it's definitely not dangerous for you—just for me and Una primarily. And Shemahn.

She uncrossed her arms.

Five minutes, and if I'm not convinced, then I'm out the door—and it'll be a long, long time before you see me again.

I couldn't stop myself from hugging her.

I promise you it won't take even that long. Come over to the dining room table so we can show you the evidence.

Less than five minutes later, after listening to Una and peeking through the shades, Hildy had decided this time was different. This wasn't her delusional dad, this was the real *Yojimbo*. Five minutes after that, she had the scripts in her bag and had walked to the door to put the rest of the plan in motion. Then she hesitated. She should have been walking out, but something was bugging her. She turned back.

What about Petunia?

What about her?

I asked.

She'll be in Angel's way. And after that, it won't be safe for her in here.

Hildy was right. We hadn't written a part for Petunia after using her to get to Hildy.

Maybe I should take her. We could pretend it was an emergency and carry her to the car.

I started to pick the dog up and then stopped myself.

No. I would go with her if it were an emergency. Taking Petunia now would make them suspicious.

What if you came back for her?

Una said.

Tomorrow. After we leave. No one would be the wiser.

Good. That'll work.

Hildy was relieved. She turned to go. Una held out a piece of paper with a phone number on it.

What's this?

A lawyer. Don't use your phone or one at the clinic. Borrow someone's and call him. Tell him Una gave you the number. And that I want him to help. He'll look after your brother.

Hold on a second

I said as I tried to take back the paper.

Hildy wouldn't let me have it.

Atticus can't just have any old lawyer

I said

Who is this guy?

He's not any old guy. He's my brother—and he's the best criminal defense lawyer in town.

Hildy looked down at the number.

Did my father tell you what Peck did?

Tried to kill him.

After he shot my vet tech. A Cuban immigrant. And he killed a couple of dogs. My brother's a racist. And he might be unhinged.

Doesn't matter.

Your brother going to feel the same way?

Racists need lawyers too.

Hildy put the paper in her pocket.

Good luck, Dad. Una, hopefully one day we'll meet under better circumstances.

She sounded like a Hollywood cliché as she opened the front door, stepped out onto the porch, and said her lines:

You were right to call me, Dad. You saved her life.

I said my line:

I couldn't have done it without you.

That shot I gave her will lessen the pain and get her through the night.

I hugged her and kissed her on the forehead.

Thanks, honey. I really appreciate your going to all this trouble for me.

I'll stop by in the morning to check on her.

She hugged me back before heading to her car. The Upgrades were taking pictures of her with their cell phones. When they looked up and saw me watching, I flipped them off and went back into the house.

Why'd you do that?

I asked.

Una was using the scanner on her phone to preserve all the emails and memos from her basket. She didn't look up.

Didn't want you thinking you were the only one who was willing to reach across the color line and help people.

I stood for a minute.

I hope you don't end up regretting it.

Not a chance. Even if it's just for the satisfaction of knowing there's a racist walking into the courtroom and realizing his lawyer's a black man.

It was gallows humor, but we still shared a laugh.

I crawled back under the house to finish the rigging. It was a race against the daylight since I wouldn't be able to use a flashlight once the sun went down. Rigging in the dark would be slower and much more difficult. And it was pretty slow to begin with since I couldn't use any power tools.

When I came up out of the hole after midnight, I'd been going for more than eight hours without a break. The worst part of it was over. I grabbed a quick PB&J, checked in on Una—who was asleep—and then got back to it.

At around five, the house was ready. I went around one last time and checked that everything I had done was clearly mapped for Angel and his guys. I put the plan in the middle of the dining room table under the spool of three-eighths wire rope they'd need and tried to make myself presentable for the day. I was sitting on the sofa, barely able to stay awake, when Una sat down beside me. Hildy's Samson robe had been exchanged for the freshly washed biking outfit Una had arrived at my door in.

All set?

She asked.

Absolutely. All we have to do now is wait for them to come get us.

You think it'll work?

It has to.

Yep

She said.

By the way, I found a text from my brother when I woke up.

And?

I'll read it to you.

She scrolled through her phone and then read aloud:

No record of individual in question being arrested or in police custody. Confirm facts please.

What the fuck?

Yeah.

I'm sure Hildy told him he shot her vet tech. And he killed two dogs. Those are the facts. Hildy and I saw them haul him away in handcuffs. The guy he shot is still in the hospital.

She thumbed out a message to her brother.

I'll have him dig some more. He probably needs to just get off his ass and go find the cops who arrested him.

This is America—not some goddamned banana republic. How does someone disappear in police custody?

You're asking me?

She wasn't laughing. She thumbed another text to her brother.

By the way, I googled Milt Milton while you were under the house.

Oh yeah?

You were right. That's not his real name.

Oh?

Yeah, nobody knows for sure, but the internet thinks he's actually Charles Coughlin, born in New Madrid, Missouri. Controversial guy.

He definitely pushes people around out here.

Not just in Hollywood. His background's controversial too. Mostly unsubstantiated. Some people say he came out of military intelligence. That he was an interrogator at Gitmo under Bush the Second. Other people say he ran the cyberwarfare arm of the NSA in the first Obama administration. Bottom line is no one knows where he came from or how he got so much power in the entertainment business.

Funny, I'd always assumed he was someone's nephew.

Definitely not. From what I read, no one wants Milt Milton in their family.

Una relayed all this without emotion. For me, it was sobering to think of what we were up against. She seemed unfazed. She closed her eyes and leaned her head back like she was going to nod off.

I had heard it was always smart to grab whatever shut-eye you could in crisis situations like this. Even fifteen minutes

could do a lot to help you survive. I decided to join her—
until I heard her laughing quietly to herself.

What's so funny?

She did not open her eyes; she just smiled her crooked little
smile.

I was just wondering why your daughter thought I was
your girlfriend.

I turned a hot red, but I did not move.

What's that about, Samson?

I don't know. You'll have to ask her.

Do you think it's because white people think black women
have such low self-esteem that we'll take any man we can
get—even an over-the-hill bald guy who's got at least a
decade on me? You know, I'm a fully developed human
with a life. I have a kid in college.

You're married?

Divorced. What is with your daughter? You think she'd
fuck an old black man? Maybe—

She seemed to be winding herself up pretty good, so I interrupted.

Maybe Hildy just assumed that any woman, of any color, walking around her father's house in a bathrobe with his nickname on it in the middle of the day would have to be his girlfriend.

That stopped her. She opened her eyes wide, mock indignation.

You haven't forgotten you gave it to me, right?

No. I haven't. If they'll let you have anything soft in prison, it's yours.

Funny.

She cocked her head to one side.

Now that we're partners, let me ask you something. I've known a lot of white men in my life, some were college educated, some not, some professionals, some not. I worked in marketing right out of college. The one thing seems to me these guys had in common—I'm talking the straight ones—is that they could hardly keep their shit together around me. It was like a nonstop question running across their LED foreheads: I want you. Let's fuck. I want you. Let's fuck. They put me in this tiny box of their privilege and wouldn't let me out. I've always wondered why that was. Why do white men think they can do that to a person?

I didn't know what to say. She pushed herself up on one elbow to face me. She took her right hand and placed her palm in the middle of my chest.

Okay. Never mind that, but tell me this. How's a person get so privileged that there's never any consequences for the shit he does?

I felt the heat of her skin through my T-shirt. Why this again? I wondered, then gave it my best shot.

I don't know. Personally, I feel like my life is made up entirely of consequences.

I looked down at her hand.

But while we're talking consequences, what are the consequences for a superintelligent, drop-dead gorgeous African American woman putting her palm in the middle of the chest of an-over-the-hill-bald-guy-who's-got-at-least-a decade-on-her? Twice?

Una looked down at her hand, turned it over, cupped it, flexed her fingers, and then tapped her knuckles gently on my sternum. It was like her hand was doing her thinking. She smiled at me, and her smile widened until it turned to a grin and laughter. She rubbed her hand on my chest in a playful way and then pushed us apart.

I was just fucking with you, Samson.

That's your privilege.

Suddenly all the playfulness was gone.

I don't think you have a clue what that word means. Privilege is some liberal white man just 'calling it like he sees it' without any real consequences. A black person will never have that privilege in this country.

She sat back on the sofa and closed her eyes again. Maybe she slept. I didn't.

I heard the sirens from a long way off.

Picture's up

I said quietly.

She was on her feet in an instant, picking up the unchained bicycle basket with both hands.

When the motorcade pulled up in front of the house, we were out the door and in the midst of it before it came to a complete stop: six off-duty LAPD motorcycle cops, two in front and four in back, and an insert car with a process trailer carrying a red Jaguar convertible. The four motorcycle cops in back angled their bikes in around the Upgrades' Suburban to wedge them in. The insert car driver got out of the cab and talked to me and the lead cop for long enough to confirm the route.

Una and I climbed into the Jag, tooted the horn twice, and the motorcade took off again. I would have liked to have seen the look on the Upgrades' faces as we drove away, but I didn't want to turn around and spoil the gag.

We headed east and north from Mar Vista, winding our way through residential neighborhoods in Santa Monica and West LA. We put on quite a show with our little parade—even for a jaded community that had seen its fair share of movie shoots. Maybe it was the fact that we had Shemahn's greatest hits blasting from the speakers on the back of the trailer.

When we got to Shemahn's house, I had to climb down to punch in the gate code. I hadn't said anything to Una, but I was counting on Milton and Ja'K not being detail oriented enough to remember that Shemahn had given me the code early on in our partnership. 'In case you need to save me again,' she had joked.

My luck held, and the gates peeled open in front of us. With sirens wailing, we roared down the long drive toward her mansion. It was also lucky that all the commotion brought Shemahn out of the house. I had counted on her wanting to see the show for herself, and she didn't let me down. She laughed as she ran down the steps and hugged me before I could climb down off the trailer.

You're crazy Samson! Does this mean you aren't mad at me?

I could never be mad at you!

I said.

I know how these stories go. By the way, you remember Una from Blacks Only.

Sure

Shemahn said, hugging and kissing her too—even though I knew she didn't.

What are you doing here, Agonistes? We told you that you were off the picture.

Ja'K scuttled up and tried to insert himself between Shemahn and me. He was on the phone.

Try his hotline, Tiffany.

He turned to me and hissed

You're a trespasser.

I grabbed the phone out of his hand and threw it into a fountain by the front door.

You're such a comedian, Ja'K. We're not trespassers. We have the gate code.

Besides, trespassing is the ultimate publicity

Una added.

I pulled him up onto the insert car

Come on. I'll show you how to play the director.

Una huddled with Shemahn to tell her the plan.

While I was getting Ja'K situated on the insert car, using Una's bike lock and chain to make sure he couldn't get loose, I watched Shemahn closely for her reaction to the conspiracy. I was slightly worried that I had misread her expression at the news conference—pinned too much hope on what I saw as her obvious suspicion of Milton and Ja'K— but I hadn't. As soon as Una finished explaining the whole plot, Shemahn climbed up next to Ja'K and got him to forget about calling Milt for his approval.

Let's just go with it, Ja'K. Have some fun

She said as she hugged him

Make sure you're buckled in tight. I can't afford to lose my director.

She jumped from the back of the insert car onto the process trailer then stopped to let us take a picture in front of the Blacks Only banner made from a bedsheet we'd just strung up. Once Shemahn and Una were in the Jag, we were ready to roll.

That's your cue, Ja'K

I shouted from where I was harnessed to the speed rail near the front of the car.

Cue?

He was nervous and excited.

You're the director. Direct!

Action!

He screamed through the bullhorn.

Two toots—and we're rolling

I shouted. Shemahn honked twice, the insert car driver honked twice, and we were underway.

A few moments later, we emerged from Shemahn's gate. Shemahn and Una were in the front seat of the picture car. Ja'K was glued to the monitors. I was harnessed to the speed rail near the front so I could keep an eye out for bogies. The Upgrades, three pairs of clones in three identical Suburbans, tailed us all the way down Beverly Glen.

Every few blocks, Ja'K would jab at something on the monitors and blast a question or an instruction at one of us through the bullhorn. We would gesture like we understood and then go back to what we were already doing. What were we going to say? Not the truth. That it was all pretend? That we weren't recording? That those were just Go cams hooked up to generate a feed for him to pretend with? That we were putting on a show to create cinematic immunity and save Shemahn's life?

'Course I have to hand it to the wannabe—he picked up the lingo pretty quick. Every so often, he'd click the bullhorn and say

Great, great, great, that's great. Now one more just like it, but pull it back just a smidge.

It was all we could do not to pee our pants laughing.

Shemahn really got into her part too: waving at people in their cars, blowing kisses at the news choppers overhead, and making the most out of being recognized and tied to Blacks Only.

A couple of times, I stopped the insert car so that fans could get their pictures taken with her in front of the banner.

Adolescent girls of all shapes and sizes were climbing all over the insert car. I was so busy running around helping kids on and off that I almost forgot about the Upgrades. And they did almost get left behind. We had so many cars following us, weaving in and out and trying to get pictures of Shemahn that they had trouble keeping up. One of the Upgrades ran a red light at Wilshire to catch us, barely missed getting T-boned by a bus and then got pulled over by a real cop who'd been following the parade since we crossed Sunset.

We took Beverly Glen all the way down to Pico and then turned east to head toward the Fox lot. When we turned in at the truck gate, the guard waved the insert car through but stopped everyone behind us. The motorcycle cops parked by the guard shack to keep the Upgrades from trying to force their way onto the lot while we prepared for the next scene. We tucked the whole rig behind Stage 7 out of sight of the news helicopters.

Two toots, and we're stopping!

Wait, wait, wait

Ja'K said through bullhorn

I haven't said cut!

The insert car had already stopped, but we all froze.

Cut! Great stuff people!

I quickly unbuckled myself and helped Shemahn and Una out of the Jag.

Angel's best boy and crew swarmed over the trailer to get the car off as quickly as possible.

Shemahn, Una, and I were going over the plan when Ja'K noticed he'd been forgotten.

What's going on, Samson?

He blasted me through the bullhorn.

You're finished in picture, Ja'K.

I'm sorry, Samson, but you have that backward. There were creative differences. There was a deadline, remember?

Ja'K struggled to get out of the harness.

The deadline's tomorrow if I'm not mistaken.

Samson's right. He has another day

Shemahn wagged her finger at Ja'K.

Show her the pages

I said to Una, who was already pulling them out of the bicycle basket.

This is half of what you asked for. Once we're clear about where Samson Productions fits in and have cleared up our creative differences, Una and I will show you the other half.

Hold it! Hold it! What about me?

Ja'K was like a kid on the wrong side of the fence watching his best friend eating an ice cream cone.

Don't read that! Don't read that! She can't read anything before I approve it.

Shemahn finally rejected her assistant's gatekeeping.

I never said you could read Samson's script before me—so calm the fuck down.

Sorry, Ja'K, better luck on the next one

I said as I checked to see that the trailer was unhooked from the insert car and gave the driver the key to Una's padlock.

Thanks, Ted. You can release our "director" over at the Holocaust Museum.

—And yes I made the air quotes in front of Ja'K—

We'll have the trailer ready and waiting for you by the time you get back.

Ja'K was still frantically trying to squirm free as the insert car headed off. You might think that the villain getting his just desserts was the happy ending we were looking for, but we weren't quite done. And if we could pull it off, the final scene promised to be a real showstopper.

You might not know this, but there are only a couple of ways to get a vehicle off the Fox lot—two gates—and you can see one of them from the other. The whole point of running to Fox was that it was not the ideal lot if you were hoping to shake a pursuer. Because we weren't. Our final scene required us running—but not getting away from—the Upgrades. We just scripted it to look that way.

We handed Shemahn off to the safekeeping of a couple of ex-Navy SEAL stunt guys I'd worked with, and then we climbed back into the Jag. Act II was a free drive with Tanya, Shemahn's stunt driver double who had rehearsed the stunt that almost killed Shemahn.

The motorcycle cops fell in around us as we sped out of gate, weaving in and out of traffic, racing ahead to block intersections, hanging back to make sure we didn't lose the Upgrades, and mostly keeping all the noncoms safe. We were all over the Westside, on the 10, on Venice.

We were lucky that Tanya was such a great driver and so into what we were doing. She did just enough crazy shit to make you wonder what was going on without really endangering anyone. I could only imagine the frustration and confusion that must have been building for the Upgrades. I mean, what the fuck was going on? It was good since we wanted them completely ready to blow.

The chase scene finally ended right back where it started: in front of my teardown in Mar Vista. The motorcycle cops sped off, leaving us alone, and we got out of the Jag as the Suburbans roared up.

Una ran through the front door and held up the bicycle basket so it was clearly visible.

I lingered on the edge of the porch long enough to watch Tanya do a doughnut in the Jag and roar off the way we'd come in.

Ashton and No-Cleft were slowly getting out of their car as if they didn't know what to do next.

I ad-libbed to motivate them.

We really led you on a wild-goose chase, didn't we?

I laughed and flipped them off.

Why don't you come and arrest us for that?

I casually turned my back and walked inside. Behind me, I could hear the sound of them charging.

Luckily, without even a half-speed rehearsal, things went flawlessly. Gags like this often have a hitch or two, nothing life-threatening—okay, sometimes life-threatening—but mostly it's just about something not going exactly the way you expected. In this case, with my pal Angel doing the rigging, the only wild card was the Upgrades' performance. We were not disappointed. And even better, the whole thing was recorded for posterity.

All six Upgrades charged through the door with their weapons drawn, apparently catching Una and me in the act of stuffing the stolen documents into the bicycle basket.

Fuck you, Samson. We're taking you and this bitch down.

Them catching us was Una's cue to blow the air mortar that filled the house with Fuller's earth and foam fragments.

As the six of them waved their arms, coughed, and gagged, Una ran out the back door. I could see the red laser sights from their guns arcing through the dusty air, but I wasn't worried about being shot. There wasn't any chance these clowns out of *The Shakiest Gun in the West* would pull the trigger. Plus, I planned to be out of there before the dust cleared. I turned on the wild animal sound effects and tripped the rig that dropped the floor of the living room like a trapdoor.

The Upgrades landed on their asses in my crawl space as the weed whackers started slapping at their legs and the screaming of rabid raccoons filled the crawl space. The Upgrades freaked out, trying to get away from the imaginary raccoons and get to me at the same time.

I pulled the cable that turned the rest of the floor into the equivalent of a thin sheet of ice on a lake, collapsing all the floorboards as soon as anyone put any weight on them.

No-Cleft stood up and found me with the red laser sight of his handgun.

You're a dead man, Samson!

I looked down at the red dot on my chest and thought for a second how different it was from Una's palm, but I didn't dwell on that comparison long enough for him to find the nerve to pull the trigger. I pushed the button on the ratchet that jerked me straight through the house and out into my backyard as the bungalow collapsed.

Of course, you're probably thinking, I'd just used my house to kill some innocent SAG extras. Even if they were trying to kill me, it wasn't like you could so easily get away with the murder of six human beings, but murder wasn't what we'd scripted. In fact, like it always says at the end of the credits, no one got hurt in the making of the movie. Okay, the Upgrades had some cuts and bruises. One thought he had broken his arm. Another one thought he had a concussion, but that was the least of their problems. They had a harder time explaining to the police why exactly they were in my house with unregistered weapons in the first place.

I didn't leave them hanging out to dry.

This is a film set. Those are stunt guys

I said to the LAPD officers, Hicks and Johnson. They were not actual cops but a couple of my acting friends who entered from camera right with guns drawn when we were pulling the last of the Upgrades out of the wreckage.

I pointed at the cameras that were set up all around my yard.

Smile for the cameras, Officers.

The police shook their heads like that didn't cut it. They kept their service revolvers trained on the Upgrades.

Drop your weapons!

They're props! Props!

No-Cleft and Ashton and the rest of the Upgrades screamed, immediately dropping their guns.

Real enough to get you shot in Chicago or South Carolina

Johnson said.

You better fuckin' have permits

Hicks said to me.

Those two were the best at improvising cop-speak in all of Hollywood. With his weapon still trained on the Upgrades, Johnson kicked the discarded Glocks into a pile. Hicks did a quick pat down.

If this is a real movie, where's the prop master?

Prop *mistress*

My Ex corrected them. She was already gathering up the pile of guns, showing the empty chambers, and ejecting the clips like a pro. It was like old times with her smiling and flirting to get the job done. She might be hairdresser in real life, but she could play any part on TV.

If you'll follow me, Officers, I'll show you all the paperwork.

Hicks and Johnson walked off with her, continuing their improv.

I hate these low-budget, nonunion shows.

Terrible craft service.

I waved the medic in to wipe the Fuller's earth out of the Upgrades' eyes and ears. The six of them huddled together and looked like they'd been pulled out of a shipwreck.

Gather around, everybody. I have an announcement to make.

I was enjoying my cameo as the first AD.

Listen up! It's a bittersweet announcement I have to make, but let's have a round of applause please for the Los Angeles Department of Water and Power. Finished in picture.

The crew pressed in on the Upgrades, applauding, clapping them on the back, hugging, and giving them kisses on the cheek.

The Upgrades were stunned but also pleased, humbly accepting congratulations, proud to be recognized for their contribution. After all, no Upgrade in Hollywood history had ever heard those words spoken about him before.

Finished in picture? Really?

No-Cleft was holding back tears.

Yup, thanks to you we got it on the first take.

Finished in Picture (Not)

Did it work? Did we make cinematic immunity real? Was Una right?

Well, we aren't dead—if that's what you're wondering—but it wasn't exactly what you'd call a Hollywood ending either.

Good things came from it sure. Bad things too.

Basically, life continued. Here's how—in no particular order.

Shemahn fired Ja'K and Milton, and she gave the whole project back to me and my new partner: Petunia "Una" Biggers. Before she went into the studio to record her next album, she and Una did a media tour, sit-downs with *60 Minutes*, *Frontline*, *Access Hollywood*, and *Late Night*— detailing both the plot of her next film and emphasizing that Shemahn was going ahead with the project even though she knew that she was putting her life in danger.

I'm counting on every one of my fans to save us from the government assassins

She said

I'm publicizing this so that if I show up dead one day from a heart attack or suicide or overdose, you'll know not to believe it. You'll know I was assassinated. And then you'll decide what you're going to do about it, but the first thing is to stop believing the bullshit the government puts out to cover its tracks.

She and Una also subjected themselves to a bunch of medical tests as part of the interview, made outside doctors review their records, and submitted affidavits saying they weren't drug addicts or suicidal or in bad health. Basically, the story was told everywhere and to everyone until the two of them were safe.

Then, since we figured the publicity wouldn't hurt our movie any, Una found a reporter at the *LA Times* who took the DWP papers and put the conspiracy story on the front page. It was the biggest scandal in LA history—for a few days. Then, Detective Bigfoot fingered Dr. Lime for Dr. Martins's murder, and the DWP management scapegoated him for the whole conspiracy. Not that Una or I minded that racist nerdnick being framed, but making the whole gray water scheme a rogue operation—and the motive for the Nutty Professor's murder—kicked the shit out of our plot. Anyone who would believe that those two were criminal masterminds engaged in a torrid love affair gone sour should have had their head examined, but people did.

Just like that, the DWP slipped out of our clutches. Sure, they paid off some health claims, but as far as Una and I were concerned, they'd skated.

Okay—not entirely. After I showed the DWP executives the footage of their employees in my house waving guns around, they offered me a quick settlement. In exchange for the footage, they muscled my corrupt contractor's insurance company for the money to rebuild my house—and put on a second story. Then they dropped seven figures on Una and me.

I gave some of mine to Hildy so she could pay off her small business loans and remodel her clinic. She named the new overnight ward after Ismael and then made him a partner. And even though I knew he would never want it, I put the some of it in a trust for Atticus. I made the Ex the trustee, and she matched my cash for both kids with a bunch of shares in her CRISPR start up. And all that generosity almost had me believing we were good parents after all—until the mystery of Atticus's escaping arrest and falling off the face of the earth was cleared up.

Una and I were meeting with a contractor to look at the pile of rubble that was my house. We were standing out in front and going over plans and logistics for the rebuild. You're wondering why Una was there. You're imagining that maybe Hildy was right about us in the end. That maybe it was possible that Una changed her mind about having a relationship with an old, bald white guy. In my dreams, you know. Long story short, the contractor was Una's boyfriend. She was there to make sure he got the job.

Anyway, we were standing in my front yard when Milt Milton pulled up in a bright red, brand-new Maserati. The windows were heavily tinted, so I wasn't sure who it was, but Petunia—still coned and barely on her feet—smelled a bad guy from a long way off. She started barking as soon as the door opened.

Milton hauled himself up out of the passenger seat, extracted a broken Ja'K from the tiny back seat, and dumped him on the sidewalk.

Good morning, y'all!

Milt shouted over the barking as he waved a triangular hand at us.

Sadly, Shemahn has terminated Ja'K, and unfortunately, I don't have a place for him at MMM now that I have a new trainee. So, we were both hoping—with your bright future, Samson—that you might find a spot for him at Samson Productions. He's not very good at taking out the garbage, but he has his talents. I won't vouch for his loyalty however.

He put his hand on Ja'K's back and pushed him toward us. It felt like a prisoner exchange or a spy coming in from the cold. Ja'K stumbled toward me like the dying clown in *Octopussy*.

What was I exchanging for this pathetic Hollywood wannabee, I wondered as I said, out of pity

Sure, why not? Besides your kind of loyalty doesn't seem worth having.

Children need something to believe in if they're not going to turn out like that one

Milton said.

I'm sure Ja'K was a good kid before you got hold of him.

They're not all good kids, Samson

Milt smiled, leaned into his car, and spoke to the driver.

Want to say hello to your father, Peck?

Silence except Petunia barking.

No? Goodbye then? No?

Milt had a big piece of me in his mouth when he turned back with a fake sad smile.

You're wondering why I used my influence to do what you could never do: get your son out of jail and have his record wiped clean. Well, unlike his parents, who tried to deny his true genius by suppressing it with the expectations of that ridiculous, un-patriotic name, I see Peck for who he really is. I know what he can achieve for himself and his country. I have no doubt your son's going to be the best trainee I ever had.

He lowered himself into his sports car. The door closed, and then they were gone. I didn't bother looking after them. I went over and pulled Petunia back from the street. Una was hugging Ja'K, who seemed to be crying. Una's boyfriend pretended to be reading something on his phone. I turned to the boyfriend and said

Tell me again how you're going to keep me from being eaten alive by the raccoon.

Bad things happened with the Shemahn project too—some worse than others. After the Lime conviction, our conspiracy screenplay ran into headwinds as soon as we handed it in to the studio. As we expected, they hit us with the whole rogue-employee party line, but we stuck to our guns and pushed back. Conspiracies make good movies, particularly fictional ones.

They appeared to back off, said it was up to us and claimed it was just a suggestion, which made Una happy, but I knew was bullshit. We hadn't heard from the lawyers yet.

Then they came at us with cutting the whole transgender story line. We were biting off more than we could chew, they said, and the director they'd forced us to hire agreed.

This guy was a nobody, basically a studio hack who got the job because he could be counted on to do what they wanted.

When we agreed to cut Ja'K's character and focus on the conspiracy, the floodgates opened. We were getting lots of notes—and not just from the hack. It felt like we had to justify our story to everyone at the studio who could walk and chew gum at the same time.

Mark my words, Una

I said

It's only a matter of time before someone asks us why the main characters aren't white.

Fuck me! Are you kidding?

I wish I were.

You mean, they'd really want us to change our story so that a white woman—

Man

I clarified.

Fuck me—man—where a white man, is a founder of the Blacks Only movement?

More or less the founder. Could be indirectly. Could be an inspiration for. Remember your white savior thing with me? You thought that was my delusion. Well, guess what. Hollywood loves that character.

But this shit really happened. It's not made up. Black people died—not whites.

She slammed her laptop closed. We were sitting across the table from each other in the Samson Production office. We were full-fledged writing partners now, and that was how we worked.

By the way, I want to tell you I've decided we're gonna need one of those announcements at the end of the movie, something like—by the way, people, this shit really happened!

We don't have final cut.

So what?

That means there won't be a card that says that at the end of the movie.

Why not?

Because the studio lawyers will say it isn't true. The DWP didn't conspire to poison African Americans—some rogue employees did. The DWP will sue the studio for defamation. The studio doesn't want that.

That's bullshit. White people didn't found Blacks Only either.

Not found. *Inspired.* Sort of. Indirectly.

Not even indirectly. I'm the founder, and I wasn't inspired by whites. *Provoked* is more like it.

Of course not, but some white person has to get credit if this story's ever going to see the light of day.

What about Shemahn? I thought she could get this green-lit.

Sure, she can, but she won't get final cut either.

Fuck.

Yeah.

We should sue those motherfuckers. Make them stand up in a court of law and tell the truth.

We could sue, but we won't get our day in court. Media companies won't allow that. In my experience, they're pretty much untouchable.

That's bullshit.

Total.

Fuck this!

Una stormed out of the office.

I didn't bother pointing out that total bullshit was the coin of the realm—or that maybe we should consider working on an alternative version of Una's story, go with the tried-and-true stars getting away with murder, and call it *Cinematic Immunity*. She might have laughed.

What else? We're on our umpteenth consecutive day of red flag warnings. Now there are fires in Bel Air, Sunland, and Santa Barbara.

Oh, and I got a new hair helmet. This one says it works in half the time.

Main on End Credits

Jennifer Rowland

India Rowland

Beatrix Rowland

Jenny Parrot

Rita Lynn

Jonathan Lynn

Tim Williams

Tim Shaheen

Michael John Garcés

Amy Schiffman

Sarah Rowland

Liza Townsend

Printed in the United States
By Bookmasters